Shadow
of a
Soldier

Shadow of a Soldier

Army Tales From
An Unpublished Diary
& Other Orphan Stories

William R. Burkett, Jr.

The New
Atlantian Library

The New Atlantian Library

is an imprint of
ABSOLUTELY AMAZING eBOOKS

Published by Whiz Bang LLC, 926 Truman Avenue, Key West, Florida 33040, USA

Shadow of a Soldier copyright © 2016 by William R. Burkett, Jr. Electronic compilation/ paperback edition copyright © 2016 by Whiz Bang LLC.

This is a work of fiction. Names, characters, places, and incidents either are the product of the author's imagination or are used fictitiously, and any resemblance to actual persons, living or dead, businesses, companies, events, or locales is entirely coincidental. While the author has made every effort to provide accurate information at the time of publication, neither the publisher nor the author assumes any responsibility for errors, or for changes that occur after publication. Further, the publisher does not have any control over and does not assume any responsibility for author or third-party websites or their contents. Publisher cannot be responsible for how this ebook appears on a particular ereader device.

For information contact
Publisher@AbsolutelyAmazingEbooks.com

ISBN-13: 978-1945772092 (The New Atlantian Library)
ISBN-10: 1945772093

Shadow
of a
Soldier

Foreword

A Few Words About Orphan Stories

FIFTY YEARS AGO I was keeping an Army diary in a shirt-pocket-size three-ring binder when I wrote: *They called them "cahiers" when Camus' diaries were published. But what do I write about Bellingham? About a cynical Valkyrie Swede who is the local police reporter, pub crawling with her and a university professor of journalism and a couple other soldiers who came up here with me to describe Army journalism to his class? About the Up and Up, the Iron Bull, Shakey's for pizza, the Winter Garden? About the telegram I sent the Swede later?*

A few years later in the flower-child years I found Richard Brautigan's unusual short-story style in *Revenge of the Lawn*. I emulated his approach, going back to my notebooks for grist. One thing I never doubted since I was 14 was that I had to write. It was almost irrelevant whether anyone read what I wrote other than occasional novels. Then my favorite baseball book's author, Kinsella, coined a term for Brautigan's style: *Brautigans*. My good friend for over fifty years, Shirrel Rhoades, had "retired" to Key West and launched this imprint. He published *Mean Grey Old Morning* for me, dedicated to Brautigan and Kinsella. My short-piece output picked up dramatically with the prospect of actually being read.

I always liked the phrase *Orphans of the Storm*. When I shipped work to Shirrel for safekeeping I said file under orphans, since I have no plan. Shirrel did. Here is my first collection of orphans. I may even complete the Valkyrie's story one day.

Shadow of a Soldier

IT HADN'T RAINED in weeks. The humidity was awful. We needed one of those apocalyptic Georgia thunderstorms from my childhood rolling down the Savannah River, thunder shaking the low red hills and terrifying bolts of lightning stabbing the earth. I was back in the red clay hills of home. But I had never felt so far from home in my life.

Across the highway, like a midday mirage from a parallel universe, a barbecue shack lay in deep shadow beneath dense oak trees. Bright neon beer signs twinkled in the shade. A thread of country music drifted on the hot breeze. Life looked normal over there.

There was no shade where I was. The sun beat down mercilessly. Red dust from the tank trail grimed my sweaty face, irritated the edges of my eyes and plastered to my sweat-soaked cotton shirt. Any sensible native of this land, like those across the road in the bar, was taking cover and waiting for evening to go outside. But I had no choice. Neither did the files of sweating silent men trudging with me. All of us were dressed alike in sodden olive drab aptly named fatigues.

My shadow on the burning ground was the shadow of a soldier.

The shadow rifle on my shoulder was canted to clear the helmet shadow. Our shadows moved unevenly over rutted and gouged ridges, the spoor of tracked metal dinosaurs laid down in wet weather and hardened into red cement by the unforgiving sun. It made for difficult walking.

We trudged down a hill where a thin black sparkle of creek water crossed the track. Somebody in the other column broke ranks and scampered down. Then a second. I waited for a sergeant's bellow that did not come. Then I saw why: it was two Colombians destined for command back home, who had been attached to us for Basic Training. The sergeants weren't sure how to treat them so they left them alone.

They moved light and fast in the enervating heat, squatted to fill their inverted helmets with creek water and slapped them back on their heads. Water cascaded down them, an instant shower. They jogged back to position with the smiles of happy children. The rest of us didn't break stride or speak. There clearly wasn't much about survival the Army could teach them when they knew tricks like that. I bet their army had better sense than to march in midday heat this bad.

My own steel pot was like a broiler for my head, parboiling my brain in my own sweat. My eyes stung. My vision blurred. I had been scheduled for KP today. That appealed a lot more than an eight-mile round trip through hell. But the Army assigned too many to the kitchen. We drew straws before the company moved out. I lost. I had not dosed on required salt tablets, because I was going on KP. I was paying for it now.

Somebody barged into me. It was our very own Gomer Pyle from West Virginia, nicknamed the first week of Basic. I shoved angrily. Walk on your side of the road I snarled. He looked hurt. I *am* on my side, he said. And he was. How had I wandered across the whole damn trail? My side seemed far away. The tank trail was suddenly much wider than when we started. I listed heavily to port, as if the M-14 on my shoulder was dragging me over.

Abruptly my rifle was gone. I yelled Hey! A big arm went around my shoulders: Pete the Greek from Brooklyn. S'okay, I got it, he said. The middle of the trail was crowded all of a sudden: Pete, Gomer and the platoon sergeant. Everybody still trudged forward. But they were having a conference about me I was not invited to join. Platoon integrity, remember, the sergeant said. Everybody makes it or no weekend passes for anybody.

Gomer stripped off my web harness. Pete shouldered my rifle with his. Each took an arm. We marched right down the middle of the trail. Up ahead I saw a smudge of distant trees. Surely an illusion. But the illusion came closer. Almost there, Pete said.

The first shade we walked into hit me almost like a punch. The temperature seemed to drop twenty degrees. I heard the platoon sergeant yell fall out, smoke 'em if you got 'em. I was flat on my back without knowing how. My wiry little captain looked down at me from a great height; he wasn't more than five foot eight. Tough little guy who adorned his fatigues with airborne and ranger patches, and a combat infantryman's badge. On his right shoulder a Special Forces patch to inform you where he was assigned when he earned the CIB.

"Didn't take your salt tablets did you?" he said with some amusement from way up there in the blessed shade.

"I was on KP," I croaked.

"Take 'em now. Where's his canteen?" Gomer handed him my canteen. Somebody else handed him a handful of salt pills. They tasted awful. I choked them down in a couple gulps of water and then held a third swallow in my mouth the way I was taught before the Army. "Drink more," the captain said. I did. It seemed wasteful but I was past arguing. "Okay, enough," he said. "Brace yourself."

He dumped my whole damned canteen over my chest. Water that was lukewarm before we started hit me like ice water in November. I gasped in shock. "Heat stroke," he said. "Got to get your temperature down. You'll be okay when the salt kicks in."

Amazingly enough I was. When we moved out on the second half of our little jaunt I was already clear-headed and steady on my feet. The sun didn't even seem as hot.

The captain jauntily showed his still perfectly starched fatigues to the platoon sergeant. "Haven't even broken a sweat," he said. Smart-alecky little bastard. But probably a good choice for turning civilians into punji-stick fodder.

Military Police School

MIITARY POLICE candidates marching to class and singing cadence, their voices echoing from the baby hills of the Savannah River plateau, sound like young gods singing past Valhalla. But MPs sweating in a detail under the Georgia sun to spread dirt over the clay field of the company area to make the grass grow greener are like peons laboring in old Mexico under the eye of some tyrannical Don. In this case, a buck sergeant.

Listening Post

AFTER SIXTEEN WEEKS of Army training over a brutally hot summer in the red-clay hills of my native Georgia, you could say I had mixed feelings about the Army. I always hated physical exercise so it required the Army's rules and single-mindedness to force me into fitness. I went in at 208 and came out at 170. The first weeks of Basic were hellish, but by the time I was finishing MP School I could do an unreasonable number of pushups and hold my own hand-to-hand with a giant NYC cop in the judo pits.

But I had always thought the Army's purpose was to produce trained killers. I was bitterly disappointed. I knew more about killing before I got there and learned nothing of value. Rifles and pistols were confined to formal target practice on immobile targets. Attempts to train us to spot hidden targets in the brush were a joke to a veteran whitetail hunter. The night we were supposed to run a compass course through the booger woods I learned two things: one, city boys believed the woods were literally paved with poisonous snakes. Two, the designated navigator had no clue that bracing his compass on his rifle barrel would affect its bearing. Only after he admitted he was lost did I learn the problem. So I read the compass against the rifle and then away to determine the margin of error, found a dry creek bed at right angles and led us across the base of an imaginary triangle to the correct course, and we got where we were supposed to be.

In our sixteenth week, with graduation from MP School looming, our last exercise reinforced my hope none of us would wind up in hostile territory facing real killers. We were to have a night combat exercise with blank ammunition. The platoon sergeant, a wit, handed me a Prick-Six, a walkie-talkie radio, saying since I was a famous writer I could afford to pay if I broke it. We marched into the Georgia night with rifles instead of .45s because we were playing soldier not cop. Hidden cadre popped smoke grenades to disorient us and threw in shrieking artillery simulators that banged as loud as cherry bombs. My private thought was at last we were having some fun.

We scattered into smaller units under the barrage, until there was maybe half a platoon with the sergeant when he led us up a small heavily treed hill. The game was capturing the flag, he told us. We were on defense, and would be attacked by others representing guerrillas. Our job would be to secure the hill, at the top of which he would plant the target flag. He issued passwords before he deployed the men in a perimeter around the hill, in case anybody needed to move out of position. He told us the flag *always* got captured, which showed what we were up against in Vietnam.

I was assigned to a listening post outside the lines with my walkie-talkie. I liked being by myself, able to pick my own spot. It was like a hunting trip as soon as I was alone. I found what would have made a good duck blind at a juncture of two sandy roads. Since I wasn't hunting ducks I slipped in under the brush prone, and removed my steel pot because every time I turned my head it scraped on the branches. I chose the spot where I could watch the roads because city-boy guerrillas wouldn't lose their fear of snakes when they wrapped a rag around their head. After the night settled down from all the artillery simulators, and the smoke dissipated, it was quiet and still, with a bright moon.

And here came the "guerrillas" sneaking down a sandy road in the moonlight, six or eight of them. The white rags would have made head shots easy. The night was so quiet I was afraid they would hear the buzz of the radio carrier wave so I turned it off. They kept coming. Eventually they stood so close I literally could have reached out and untied one's bootlaces. They were muttering they must be close to the perimeter by now. At which point our veteran sergeant felt compelled to walk the line of defense behind me on the hill, telling everyone to be ready and remember the password was...whatever it was. I don't remember. But his voice carried plainly. Did you get that, one of the men standing on top of me said. Can it be that easy? Suppressed chuckles. Then they eased on up the hill.

I heard a sentry sing out a challenge and one of the raiders answer with the password. Then nothing. I turned the radio back on and raised the line. I said the squad that just came through using the password is the bad guys. They heard you saying it up there. Turn around and take them from behind; they won't expect it. The gunfire erupted soon after. Of course they were blanks. One of the raiders must have played guns as a kid. (I got you! Did not! Did too!) Because he came galloping back down the hill through the brush making his escape. I waited until he was too close to sheer off and rose out of my hide and fired for center-mass, close enough to smear powder from the blank on his fatigues. He yelped like he was shot for real and kept running; asshole.

He obviously told his buddies who were waiting back, because suddenly the artillery simulators started falling all around me. They fell so close I put my pot back on and cowered. I'd seen what cherry bombs can do. The barrage relented after a while and I expected them to try me again. But they didn't. Later I heard a walkie-talkie command to make "the final push." There was more shooting on the other side of the hill. Then the sergeant called us in, saying the exercise was over.

The walkie-talkie command was explained when they told me the guerrillas had captured other LPs and confiscated the radios. They failed in their final push because they tried the password trick again but word had passed around our perimeter. That was the gunfire. The sergeant was pleased because we'd held the flag. I wanted to inspect the prisoners for one with a powder-stained shirt but he said get serious. I was serious; I wanted a confirmed kill. I was back in my play-gun mindset.

After that exercise I learned I was going to Germany not Vietnam. I breathed a sigh of relief because I had a hunch the VC didn't walk openly in the moonlight. I wondered how quickly actual combat would winnow out men with only sixteen weeks of training, very little of it as close to reality as our little night exercise. Men who walked down a sand road in moonlight and thought they were sneaking.

Madison Ave
in Germany

WHEN I GOT TO GERMANY in the 1960s I thought I had escaped the reach of Madison Avenue. But no.

One of the more ludicrous aspects of German cities was that their Esso gas stations cheerfully displayed the Esso tiger. With this famous Madison Avenue banner rendered in Deutch: "Pack den tiger in den tank!"

Secret Agent Man

ASHTON WAS A GOOD-LOOKING kid, you had to admit. Had that big-city swagger too. He strutted around the Fort Jackson Army Induction Center in his civvies like he owned the place, with his Kooky Kooky Lend Me Your Comb hair styled just so. When they marched us to the Army barbers you should have seen the guy's eyes light up that got Ashton in his chair. Maybe he thought shearing Ashton would trim his attitude like Delilah took Samson's strength. Fat chance.

"Cut it away carefully, my man," Ashton instructed airily. "I've promised lockets of my hair to a number of lonely ladies back in the City."

Damned if that Army barber didn't do it, too, and swept up the blonde curls carefully and presented them to Ashton with a flourish. I had a crew cut already, but my guy leaned on my skull with the clippers like he'd been cheated. I was bald as Yul Brynner when he was through. Go figure.

I'd never seen Ashton before we were shoved into our first transient barracks together there at Fort Jackson. The way things worked out in those days, the two of us and about a platoon's worth of other draftees from all over the East Coast wound up going through Basic Training together and then to Fort Gordon Military Police School. After over sixteen weeks of living in each other's hip pockets, some of us were lifetime buddies and some of us had to be pried apart to keep us from killing each other. They called the fistfight between me and that Wop truck driver from New

Jersey the clash of the titans. Ended in a draw and we didn't shake hands and make up, either.

Ashton sailed above it all with his big city strut and smart mouth. His wisecracks were funny enough to relieve the olive-drab tedium, nothing truly memorable, just funny at the time. Drill Sergeants' harassment bullshit rolled off him like water off a duck. Even the Drill Sergeants had to laugh at his cockiness and smart mouth.

As MP School wound to a close we all hung around the day room bulletin board in spare moments, waiting for our orders to be posted. The day most of our names went up, slotted for Saigon, things got quiet around the barracks. My name was on there, and so were Ashton's and a lot of the other guys who'd been together the whole way.

Viet Nam was heating up, and it looked like we were going to be tossed into the fire as Saigon embassy guards. We knew that made us sitting ducks, even though it was before that VC bomb that took out all the windows on one side of the embassy. That blast gave a CIA guy I got to know years later a face full of glass fragments when he incautiously went to the window when he heard gate MPs shooting. He survived the experience, but decided he'd had enough and took a civil-service transfer to the U.S. Fish and Wildlife Service, an option I never even knew existed until I heard it from him.

But a bunch of us on that bulletin board never saw Saigon.

At the next company formation the first sergeant read out twenty names. Mine. Ashton's. A lot of the others who came all this way with us. We fell out and formed up on a staff sergeant we'd never seen before. He marched us away across dusty red-clay training fields to one of those stand-alone classrooms in which we'd been taught military law enforcement. An officer we'd never seen before was waiting. The staff sergeant and an SFC went around lowering blackout curtains over all the windows. It looked like we were going to be shown a movie. The captain locked the door.

"This briefing is classified Secret," the captain said without preamble. "This is an order: you will not discuss this briefing with anyone outside this room."

Then he said we'd been especially handpicked from among the best, blah blah blah. The words ran together. I didn't like this at all. The last time a lifer captain gave me a sales pitch it was because my test scores had him trying to recruit me into Officer's Candidate School and a longer tour of duty. No thank you very much. This time they weren't giving us a choice. We had already been recruited without knowledge or consent. We weren't going to Viet Nam after all. We were going to Germany. The Sergeant First Class doused the lights. The staff sergeant operated a squeaky old movie projector. For a minute it was like back in high school, about to watch an "educational" film. Then it wasn't.

We were looking at grainy black-and-white footage of old Nazi V-2 storage bunkers in a German forest. But the soldiers in the film were American, and the warheads on the rockets were nuclear.

"Your job will be to protect these missile sites from Communist infiltrators and spies," the captain intoned. "This is our real priority in the world today. Any grunt can go shoot it out with the slopes in the jungle. You have been selected to be on the front lines of the Free World." We would be the first defense against the Godless Soviet Bloc, he told us, authorized to shoot to kill. And a lot more in that vein. When we were marched back to the barracks area, Ashton was positively aglow.

"Man this is it, this is what I've been waiting for," he said. "Secret agents, man! James Bond stuff. Then he hummed a few bars of "Secret Agent Man" from that old TV series starring Patrick McGoohan. "Giving me a number, and take away my name," he crooned. Swear to God.

The rest of us thought he should get a grip. No matter what the Army promised you, there was always a catch. Somebody dubbed Ashton "Double-o" in disgust, and the moniker stuck. It didn't bother him a bit. He was insufferable from then on, suddenly full of all kinds of secret knowledge about the mission that sounded like bullshit from spy novels, and probably was. I heard that crap from Ashton all the way north on an old TWA Constellation prop job that bumped and rattled over air pockets like a stagecoach. At Fort Dix, N.J, they sequestered us "security police" away from other Army replacement troops moving through the repo depo. Then we were hustled onto a chartered 707 to Frankfurt, along with a bunch of Military Intelligence people in civilian clothes: cheap suits from J.C. Penney and Sears, Roebuck. They pulled the plane off by a hangar in Frankfurt to unload us. A buck sergeant wearing the first AWSCOM patch I had seen on his fatigues herded the MPs onto a military bus with the windows blacked out.

We off-loaded in the middle of the night into a bullet-scarred stone courtyard that must have been through a hell of a firefight in the last war. We got an interrupted night of sleep in small windowless rooms converted into four-man squad billets. They fed us in a large basement mess hall. We sat around half the day before they formed us up in the courtyard to get on the bus again. For reasons known but to Army bureaucracy, they took us off the bus on a Frankfurt street corner four blocks from the bahnhof and marched us the rest of the way, staggering under our heavy duffel bags. Then they gave us train tickets and left us alone on the platform. As far as I know, none of us spoke ten words of German.

We formed a khaki island among the thronging German civilians, slumped on our duffels, some playing cards, most of us still trying to catch up on our sleep. Mostly the Germans ignored us. A lot of them were in bright-colored sweaters, lugging skis and knapsacks. The frauleins were rosy cheeked. There wasn't a single crew cut among the young German men.

Of course Ashton had to put on a show of trying to talk to the girls. He got some smiles and a laugh or two, don't ask me how, and claimed he had at least one girl's Frankfurt phone number, in case he needed a "safe house" later. I'm telling you, he was out of control with that bullshit.

It was coming twilight again when our train was called. We loaded into first class compartments behind one of those tootling electric locomotives bound for the hinterland. The conductor had his instructions; he wouldn't let any civilians sit in our section. That got us a few dirty looks, and it also got Ashton going again. He whistled "Secret Agent Man" halfway across Germany. He did have a tuneful whistle.

Ten of us finally detrained at two in the morning at a whistle-stop town. We were collected by yet another

AWSCOM sergeant in starched and tailored fatigues, and crawled exhausted into the back of a deuce-and-a-half, tarped over like a covered wagon, for the last leg up winding mountain roads. I dozed uncontrollably to the lurch of the big truck. It was cold as hell after spending the summer outdoors in Georgia. We were miserable in summer khakis. All but Ashton, who acted like a kid on the way to Christmas.

We finally rolled through a raised checkpoint pole onto a darkened company street lined with silent barracks in the middle of a Brothers Grimm forest. The MPs on the gate were anonymous under their helmet liners, armed and silent as they watched us go by. We were in a whole different part of the Army than any of us had seen or imagined. Except Ashton, of course.

The truck stopped in front of a lighted mess hall that looked more like a civilian cafeteria than anything on an Army post. The night cook had a full breakfast laid out for us. It was actually good food, scrambled eggs, unburned toast and hash browns. The coffee smelled wonderful in the crisp mountain air. The sergeant who brought us in told us to eat all we wanted. I began to wonder if Ashton might be right, and we'd stumbled into something good. They put us to bed in a Quonset hut reserved for transient troops. The beds had inner spring mattresses, a far cry from stateside Army cots, and the curving walls were painted a soft cream instead of baby-shit green. The softer side of the Army. I went to sleep wondering if Ashton was going to have the last laugh on us doubters. They even let us have eight straight hours of sack time before they rolled us out mid-morning and told us to get into fatigues.

When we formed up in front of the Quonset hut, we could

see a lot more than when we came in. It was a misty autumn-like day, and the evergreen forest surrounding the installation was dotted here and there with the gold and red of deciduous trees, shining in the buttery German sunlight. The other end of the company street stopped against the double gates of an eight-foot-tall steel hurricane fence that came out of the forest to the left and swung away at an angle to the right before vanishing into the trees. There was concertina wire along the top of the fence. We could see two guard towers from where we stood. I could make out an M-60 mounted on the nearest one. It looked like a maximum-security prison. In our duffel-rumpled slick-sleeve fatigues and OD baseball caps we fitted right in: we looked like convicts.

A master sergeant came down the company street, his Corcoran jump boots gleaming like black glass in the sun, and called us to attention. His fatigues were so tailored and starched that even MacArthur would have approved. His sunglasses could have been filched from the Great Man's hip pocket. It was hard to believe we were wearing the same uniform. He looked us over with something approaching disgust.

"Okay," he said finally. "First, we're going to feed you lunch. Then you report right back here for painting detail, grass cutting and policing up the company area." As of that moment we were back in the Army we had come to know and loathe over the hot summer months in the scrub pine and clay hills of Georgia. I heard the sergeant say we wouldn't be assigned our permanent billets for a few days, because the men we were assigned to replace hadn't rotated home yet. He asked if anybody had any questions.

Ashton did, of course.

"I thought our mission was to guard the missiles," he said.

The sergeant snorted. "Oh, you will. Eventually. After you get your Security Clearance. First we gotta fingerprint you. We'll do that tomorrow after we get the company area policed up. Then we gotta send the fingerprint cards back to the States for the FBI to do a background check. Can't have any Commies sneaking into the ranks between MP School and here, you know." He thought that was funny, so he laughed.

"That could take weeks!" Ashton said in something like horror.

"Yep," the sergeant said, very satisfied. "Sometimes even months. Good news for me: I haven't had a work detail worth anything in months. We've got an Inspector General's inspection coming up. I've got tons of work needs done. Painting the curbs in front of the orderly room, new stripes on the gate poles, lots of brush-cutting to clear fields of fire out along the exclusion fence." He waved vaguely toward the guard towers. "Yep, lots of work. Now head on over to the mess hall. Dismissed."

I fell in behind Ashton in the chow line. "Your mission," I said, in my best imitation of the somber *Mission Impossible* voice on the tape recorder, "should you decide to accept it ..."

"Oh, go to hell," Double-O said bitterly. "Just go to hell."

Whistle Stop

TRAINS IN GERMANY run on time, no fooling. That was the first thing I learned about them. You could escape the crushing boredom of Army life for an afternoon by going off to dinner in some city a hundred clicks away as long as you didn't miss the evening train back to base. The local station was a whistle-stop across the autobahn from our Army installation; not every train stopped there.

A buddy from the 164th MPs and I enjoyed a very nice dinner in the German version of a Mexican restaurant in Landstuhl. There was a bullfight poster on the wall, and a single gaudy sombrero like they sell tourists in Tijuana. The bullfight poster was for a Spanish corrida, not Mexican, and there was nothing either country would recognize on the menu; yellow rice that looked dyed with Easter egg dye was advertised as "authentic" Spanish rice. Entrees were comfortably Hessian and the waitress was Swiss.

The restaurant was a good three kilometers from the Landstuhl bahnhof. We enjoyed talking to the pretty Swiss and stayed longer than prudent so we had to double-time back. This felt odd in civilian clothing, but didn't draw a passing glance. German trains wait for no man and Germans get it about running to catch a train. We made it aboard and collapsed into cheap seats. It was too many months from MP judo pits at Fort Gordon, Georgia. Like most cops we never voluntarily exercised after we escaped the academy. We were breathing hard.

We were on the local, stopping at every small town. They gave you five minutes to clear the train. Putnam went straight to sleep. I was afraid if I dozed we'd miss our stop. We'd eventually find our way back if we slept through, but the Army had its own rules. Given our security clearances, the command would be in a snit if we were late, suspecting we had decamped for the Czechoslovakian border. The Cold War was crazy like that.

One whistle stop before ours I saw a blonde woman in a long black winter coat step off leading a sleepy little tow-headed boy by the hand. She had that expressionless ice-cold Nordic beauty you saw in Germany. The boy stumbled slightly. She tuned and bent to him. The turned-up sable collar of her coat gapped open.

A fresh livid scar that looked like a healing knife wound cleaved her lovely chin exactly and curved under and down her otherwise flawless neck beside her jugular. It shocked me like some fiend's desecration upon an altar.

She steadied her young charge and straightened, hand going automatically to the collar to conceal her disfigurement. Our eyes met for an instant. I have seen more emotion in stone angels in cemeteries. Then the train moved on. She and the child vanished in the night. A five-minute whistle stop in Germany, but it seared an image of violence in my brain past all forgetting.

Stroll Along the Neckar

I CROSS THE BRIDGE from downtown Heidelberg and amble slowly along the road on the far side, past tidy little gingerbread houses that look cozy and snug in the persistent cold misting rain. Tourist directions indicate the Philosopher's Walk is nearby, but the directions point to streets that climb steeply from the riverbank. Sixteen blistering weeks of Army training in the summer just gone make me think more like an infantryman than a philosopher: never go climbing steep hills to reach the high ground unless tactical considerations require it.

I walk almost to the last houses downstream on this side of the river. At 1320 military time I flush that coot again from the shore-side weeds that I jumped right after I crossed the bridge. It's duck season at home. Last year about this time Earl and I were giving the coots hell on the Guano. Fulica Americana, American coots. This one probably is Fulica atra, the Eurasian coot. But he flushed downstream so I couldn't make out if his white beak was slightly more stream-lined than his American cousin's as it is supposed to be. A coot that flounders away trying to get airborne looks like a coot, period.

Chuffing barges waddle past, seagulls joyride down the river current. Back across the bridge into narrow cobbled streets downtown, past closed and dark Student Caves that last night were bright with neon and loud with music. Other strollers are out on the damp Hauptstrasse; Germans don't let a little rain interfere with their Sunday constitutional.

A girl in an orange sweater leans on her elbows at a high window gazing across the rooftops, seemingly lost in reverie. I will never know what has her so deep in thought. Another girl in a red topcoat, walking in that Teutonic quick-step; her high heels piston echoes out of the stone building fronts. Lots of girls by themselves and in small coveys, or on the arms of young German men: blondes, blondes, brunettes, more blondes. The slender males in their bulky rollneck sweaters manage to look effeminate even with their full sea-captain beards and a statuesque blonde on their arm.

Pulling Alert

THE ARMY, like all institutions, has a vocabulary all its own. In the long dreary Cold War decades after Hitler's Reich collapsed, the East and West were eyeball to eyeball, like deranged gamblers, across the poker table of a partitioned Germany. The Army had a term called "pulling alert."

In the hierarchy of paranoid fears that the other side might flip a card face up at any moment, there were several stages of alert, ranging downward from all-out. That was where every soldier was deployed to defensive positions in the field, even the clerks. Telephone calling trees were used to assemble dependents for evacuation. Those drills were mercifully rare. The mildest form of alert required that a certain number of troops, normally off-duty for the night, stand by in battle dress, ready to mobilize and double the standing watch in under half an hour. This duty was democratically rotated through all unmarried soldiers. When your name came up, it was a lost night of drinking and playing pinball machines in the enlisted men's club. No small sacrifice those dreary German winters, when drinking and pinball were the only recreation.

So why would I volunteer for another dry night, on behalf of a man who could not return the favor? Why would any of us in headquarters platoon do that for this man? We were all cynical draftees who never volunteered for anything.

The man for whom I stood watch was Regular Army, not a draftee. He was a gentle giant of a man, whose whole ambition in life was an Army career, a "lifer" in the sarcastic jargon of us draftees. He was an excellent military cop. Those of us in the Military Police Company who had been civilian cops said that any police force in the world would be lucky to have him. He was a steady, solid worker, fearless; but he exercised his authority over others with humility and common sense.

He re-enlisted for enough bonus pay to make a down payment on a new Volkswagen. Not your most ambitious man.

But he was in love. Deeply, irrevocably in love with a German girl whose misfortune it was to have been born in East Germany, the Communist-owned half of the divided nation. She was the mother of his one-year-old son. He stayed off-post with her every night. But the Army paperwork that would permit a marriage was bogged down somewhere, and might stay bogged down forever. Because he might be sleeping with the enemy.

This particular night he was, anyway.

Because, though it was his turn on alert, I sat in the beer-free snack bar in my soldier costume and drank coffee. I wanted a beer, badly.

But I felt virtuous. And so did everybody else who aided this love, even the lifers in command. Procedure required them to authorize substitutions on the alert roster. I typed the damn thing. Never once did they question it when I penciled in another name against his. We all knew what they were doing to him was typical Army chicken shit. So we joined the open conspiracy, cynical draftees and lifers together, to ensure that one man who had found his woman could spend every possible moment with her.

The unit commander, a former football star somewhere, had called in a favor at headquarters to prevent this particular soldier from being rotated stateside when he re-enlisted. But the C.O. could not "designate" him as married, as he was permitted to do for others with long-standing relationships with German women, because of the question mark over his lady's East German origins.

In the weird looking-glass war of intelligence and counter-intelligence, the powers that be weren't about to let a Soviet sleeper agent use wedding vows to corrupt a Midwestern Specialist Fourth Class with a NATO Final Secret Clearance. How the moles in Langley must have laughed up their sleeves.

We all knew it was bullshit. But if he was designated as married, the unmarried enlisted men living in the barracks would have to pull more alerts and miss more beer-drinking time. One of them, already jealous because he had a steady shack job, might write a letter to his Mommy, and she might tell a Congressman. The glare of indignity over a curly-haired draftee missing his beer because a shambling, inarticulate lifer was in thrall to Soviet pussy could have been terminal to the C.O.'s own ambitions.

The gentle giant might still be transferred out one day, before the marriage papers cleared. The papers might never clear the Red-fearing red- tape pushers. He might never be able to make it back to Germany for her. It might

all end in that relatively minor tragedy, to anyone except the participants, of true love, lost for good.

I sat in the snack bar, sober as the mythic judge.

Tonight he was sleeping her warm. It was all I could do.

The Chocolate Debt

GERMANY HAS AN awful lot of scenery for such a small country. Back when the Cold War was really chilly, we got to see a lot of its western regions. We were a security company of Military Police, riding shotgun on convoys that carried nuclear warheads around the countryside. Ordnance was constantly shifting the stuff around from launch pads to bunkers and back again. The general idea was to keep the SovBloc from knowing where enough of it was at any one time to risk a preemptive strike.

Ordnance would lay on ten tractor-trailers, for example, and maybe five of them had warheads under the tarps and maybe three of them did; the rest were decoys. We wore steel pots and plain fatigues, nothing to identify us as MPs. We carried M-14s instead of .45s, with four full magazines of 7.62 NATO ball ammo strapped to our waists. No magazine in the rifle; the Soviets were accustomed to watching our infantry play war games all over West Germany. The infantry never had magazines locked and loaded out on the autobahn, and no one could see inside our ammo pouches. We duct-taped the unit designations on the bumpers of our vehicles to conceal our identities.

Because the Soviets helped whip Hitler in World War Two, they got to drive around just about anywhere they wanted in West Germany. We'd see the black SovBloc sedans up on the autobahn overpasses, and wave to the men in bulky overcoats lugging heavy field glasses. Sometimes they'd wave back.

The Army truck drivers were a lonely bunch and usually garrulous, not unlike over-the-road truckers back home. When you rode shotgun with one, you always got to hear his life story before the end of the run. They liked to do what they called public relations work with the civilian population as they double-clutched through the small towns and villages, waving at kids and the pretty frauleins. We got plenty of waves and happy smiles back from the pretty frauleins when we were on the road. But I had mixed feelings about all the friendly waving. My Georgia grandmother always hated the Krauts, and I guess some of her animosity stuck to me.

She lost her fiancée to mustard gas in France during the First World War. Her supervisor on the telephone switchboard sent her home to grieve in private when she got the telegram. Her mother sneered at her and sent her right back to work. The fiancée had been from Maryland and therefore almost a Yankee; not worth a Georgia girl's tears. After that my grandmother married the first man she could find to take her out of her mother's house, and always blamed the Krauts for her unhappy marriage. By the time she raised two sons and a daughter to adulthood, the Krauts got at her again.

Her oldest she figured for at least President of the United States. But he came back from Eisenhower's staff enamored with the military and turned into a lifer whose highest rank was Brigadier General – not quite the White House. She blamed the Germans and the war.

Her middle child was the strong son, the brave one; he came back with a chest full of hero medals but all his bright curly hair had thinned and straightened and faded. He limped on painful legs full of German metal that made him groan and sweat his bed, and that the VA Hospital never fixed right. His combat nightmares made it necessary to poke him with the long end of a broom to wake him up for work, or risk evisceration with the bayonet he was never without. Of course his problems were the Germans' fault.

Their sister, my mother, married a shy GI from Arkansas she saw in a parade downtown, and of whom my mother approved, calling him the sweetest young man she had ever met. I was born the year before he went ashore at Normandy with the Fourth Division, and started earning nightmares of his own.

My mother divorced him as soon as the war was over, when her brothers caught him sleeping with the wife of one of his wounded buddies, who was still in a military hospital. My grandmother didn't blame his double betrayal on his weak character; she blamed the Germans for ruining his sweet nature.

My grandmother's hatred for the Krauts grew to a fever pitch after V-E Day, fanned by watching black-and-white newsreels of victorious GIs being swarmed by German urchins. The GIs gave the kids real chocolate bars and real rubber balls that bounced. In the States, everything was still being rationed. I was a cranky baby; I wouldn't nurse and I wouldn't drink plain cow's milk. My rake-hell grandfather traded black-market stockings that he'd acquired for his roadhouse girlfriends for bootleg Hershey's chocolate syrup to sweeten my milk. I flourished on chocolate. It was one of the few redeeming acts of his life, according to my grandmother.

Those newsreels in the movie theaters, showing GIs fraternizing with enemy spawn, were the final outrage for my grandmother. Kraut kids getting better treatment than her first precious grandson. Little rattlesnakes get big rattlesnakes, she would mutter darkly as we waited for the Gene Autry double-feature at the Modjeska to start. She was an iron-willed woman from a family with plenty of practice at hating, beginning with Reconstruction and Carpetbaggers.

Germany seemed so large and real and rural out on the autobahns, after a childhood colored by my grandmother's unrelenting icy rage at Germans. The sun would enflame the dusky autumn hills and nearly perpendicular vineyards; farming villages were strewn like gingerbread blocks along narrow ribbons of pavement in the rolling hills. There were narrow cobbled streets and quaint church steeples in every little town.

It seemed unreal that my crippled-up infantry uncle had shot a German sniper out of one of those steeples who had been leisurely picking off wounded GIs trapped in a minefield. A Georgia squirrel hunter using iron sights against a trained Nazi sniper with a scoped Mauser; the poor treed Kraut never had a chance.

My grandmother liked to sit in her old wicker rocker and open the daily mail with the JugendKorps dagger my uncle took off the corpse at the foot of that church steeple. She would stroke the hilt and smile, and smile...

Between the scattered West German towns, vast vistas of peaceful valleys and foothills rising to mountains that always seemed to have clouds anchored on their peaks. I saw cows used as beasts of burden on the rural farms, and chugging tractors gathering the yield of orderly fields that stretched with German precision over almost every inch of arable soil. The harvesters in their baggy clothing with bandannas around their heads, men and women toiling together, bore no resemblance to the war-movie Krauts who killed her fiancée in that first war and that my father and uncles killed in the second.

My grandmother didn't think that chopping Germany in two was enough damage; she thought the whole country should be disassembled into its component bits and those bits watched like a hawk, until we had an excuse to start killing them again. She had no doubt they'd get up to no good and provide an excuse. She thought it was a terrible foreign policy blunder to side with even half of Germany against the Russians. She admired the Russians because they had done some serious German killing of their own under the supreme command of a different kind of Georgian. She liked it that the Soviet Union had a Georgia of its own whose famous son had filled so many German graveyards.

I thought about her obsessions a lot on our convoy runs. This particular trip I'm remembering, we were taking a ten-truck convoy on an autobahn detour around Saarbrucken to further confuse the Soviets before we scooted for silos on the Czech border. Winter was really setting in; it was cold and dank at midday, with fog so thick the trucks ahead and behind me were almost invisible. The German traffic whizzed by us on all sides like demented insects. We heard over the two-way that the lead jeep had stopped in a zebra-striped safety zone at an off-ramp to make sure we went the right way, and then all hell broke loose.

My driver cursed a blue streak when the brake lights of the trucks ahead came on all at once, and jammed his own brakes on. It was a close thing. I tucked my head, expecting to get rear-ended. When that didn't happen, we bailed out into the fog.

Warwick, the MP sergeant from the lead jeep, was half jogging down the shoulder.

"Set up a perimeter," he grunted. "Both sides. We're going to be here a while."

"What happened, Sarge?"

"Some damn 'rad tried to take the off-ramp too fast and flipped his car. He's wheels-up back there by my jeep, yelling whiplash. Guess he sees a big liability settlement from Uncle Sugar. Keep gawkers away!" He jogged on down the line.

I wound up holding a spluttering road flare at the tail end of the convoy, waving it at cars to push them into the middle lane as they came too fast out of the fog. Some of them hit their brakes and skidded a little on the skin of ice the fog was laying down. I thought this would be a hell of a way to die for the good old U.S.A., run down by a gawking comrade. That's what we called all Europeans, 'rad for short. God knows what they called us. The German cops who responded to the accident strutted around in high-peaked caps like Nazi generals, too busy "investigating" to help with traffic control.

Hotch and Sweetham were back there with me, keeping away onlookers drawn up onto the autobahn by the sirens. Sweetham was some character. He was trying to get the kids to get a soccer ball so they could kick it back and forth along the shoulder. They got over to him in sign language that their soccer ball was busted. The kids thought the wreck was just grand, but big Army trucks and steel-pot-wearing GIs with rifles were even grander. They wanted to climb in the trucks. We nixed that. Then they wanted to hold our rifles. They settled for looking Hotch's over while he held it out for them to inspect.

I was feeling pretty odd with all those Kraut kids out there on the shoulder of the road. First I thought it was the danger, then I remembered my grandmother and those black-and-white newsreels. Our uniforms in the 1960s weren't that different from World War Two. With our steel pots and shapeless OD parkas in the washed-out, colorless day, it was almost like watching one of those newsreels. Our M-14s, without magazines, looked a lot like the Garand battle rifle they replaced. American soldiers hadn't yet started carrying black plastic rifles that looked like Mattel toys or wearing Kevlar headgear with an uncomfortable resemblance to Nazi helmets.

Each time the traffic lulled I would glance around to see if anybody noticed how nervous I was. It was as if my grandmother might be looking over my shoulder. That's when I saw the little old German lady coming up to Hotch. Her hair was like spun snow, drawn into a neat little bun with a pin. She looked like tintypes of my great-grandmother, the one who hated Yankees as virulently as my grandmother hated Krauts. She was so tiny she looked like one of those little cuckoo clock figures come to life. She wore a black shawl over a long dark dress, dark woolen stockings and carpet slippers, and she walked really slowly. Her face was berry-brown and eroded by God knew how many seasons of tough living. But her eyes were bright and sparkling blue jewels that gave the lie to age, weariness or any bitterness toward the living or the dead.

The boys all smiled at her and shouted to her something about the Amerikanishen and she nodded and smiled, smiled and nodded. She didn't have any teeth.

"What you got there, Grandma?" Hotch said.

She smiled and nodded some more, and said something back in German.

Sweetham was our translator. "She wants to give us something," he said. "A gift."

With what amounted to a ceremonial flourish the little old lady produced a flat brown-paper-wrapped package from her shawl, and handed it to Hotch.

I felt a funny little clench in my belly and unsnapped one of my ammo pouches. I guess I read too many James Bond books in those days, because my first thought was that this whole situation could be some kind of trap to get at what we were carrying. They didn't issue us all that ammunition just for the hell of it. We had enough nukes along that day to level three or four big cities and we had all had the briefings about rich-kid German terrorists who might try to cause a major incident.

"What is it, Sweetham?" Hotch was fumbling with the package.

"Damn fool," I said. "It could be a bomb."

She cocked her head at me. Her eyes went uncertain. She heard the distrust.

Hotch saw it, too. "Ah, shaddup, you moron," he said. "You scared her!"

"It's just chocolate," Sweetham said. "Open it up, Hotch."

Hotch peeled back the wrapper. "Damn. That's what it is!" He passed it under his nose and made a lip-smacking sound. The kids laughed. The little old lady started smiling again, and bobbing her head. Hotch carefully broke off a chunk and tasted it. "Oh, man. This is the real stuff."

I kept my mouth shut and waited for him to go into strychnine convulsions. He didn't. He broke off a chunk for Sweetham. Sweetham nibbled a small piece and said something to the old woman that puffed her up and got her eyes really sparkling again. She ducked her head and nodded, nodded and ducked her head, and then started rounding up the kids and shooing them back off the shoulder of the autobahn toward the village. Hotch and Sweetham watched them go, gnawing on the chocolate.

Sergeant Warwick came back along the line to tell us the wreck was almost cleared, and we would be able to move soon.

"What you got there?" he asked Hotch.

"Some real by-God German chocolate," Hotch said. "An old lady gave it to us. Want a chunk?"

"Hell, yes! I could use it!" He went back up the line munching cheerfully.

I doused the flare in the roadside dirt and rubbed my hands on my parka. The hand that hadn't held the flare was numb from the cold.

"You gonna have a chunk of this?" Hotch said.

"I like chocolate fine," I said. "Ever since I was a baby."

I couldn't help but think that maybe that little old woman had watched those same combat GIs my grandmother had seen on the newsreels, being generous with their chocolate to half-starved German kids. Now, twenty years later, maybe she had made her small gesture to repay a chocolate debt.

"Have a chunk," Hotch said.

"Thanks." It had that dark wonderful smell of the best chocolate on earth.

"Anything wrong with you?"

"Not a thing," I said, and started up the line to my truck.

I gave the chocolate to my driver. I wish I could have got my grandmother to believe my sentimental notion about the chocolate debt, but her mind had been made up long ago about Krauts. And I could never have faced her again if I so much as tasted German chocolate handed to me in a sepia-toned rerun of those newsreels that fanned her hate so hot.

USO Show

IT'S TEN P.M. The Brothers Grimm woods surrounding this little Army installation in Germany are a vast black silence into which the hopeful music of a USO band is absorbed like a sponge. The USO show rolled in just now, delayed by an alert that shut down all military movement for a while. They went straight to work. The electric guitars wail and the drums throb and a live female's singing voice has an erotic effect on me that I would not have believed in the innocence of my lost civilian-hood.

Perhaps because it is the first live female voice I have heard in over a month that did not emanate from one of the 50-year-old Kraut mama-sans who pull KP for us. We each have six bucks deducted from our meager monthly soldier's pay to get out of KP. It's worth it; but objects of sexual interest they are not.

I was leaning in the door of my Quonset hut barracks smoking a sixty-five-cent aluminum-shank pipe I bought with a package of Mixture 79 in Heilbronn, where I went to cash a check at the American Express. A brassy blonde in a screaming red crinoline came out the back door of the club for a smoke break, espied me across the company street, and gave me a big wave and a smile. Probably thirty-six or so, she's over the hill but not around the bend; certainly attractive enough for the Deutchsticks.

I waved back, but did not cross the street to view the show. For some reason I cannot now recall, I swore an oath upon an old *Bob Hope in Korea* TV show that I would never attend one of these farces to become another clichéd horny GI face in the crowd.

Three Ways to Adjust

SMYTHE AND TRIMBLE coined the phrase that there are only three ways to adjust to life in the Big Green Machine, aka United States Army: the Arms Room, the Mail Room and Karlsruhe Beer.

Smythe selected the mail room because mail clerks somehow escaped all the chicken shit in a Military Police company captained by an up-tight lifer. His sandy hair was too long and never combed, his fatigues sloppy, and he wore the issue .45 with which he protected our mail slung low like a gunfighter from his home state Arizona. And he got away with it. Trimble chose the arms room because you don't mess with the armorer if you want your gun to function when you really need it. Both spent all their off-time soaking in Karlsruhe and cursing the Army.

Smythe claimed to have a poet's soul, and played loud flamenco guitar in the squad room. But in a rare moment of candor he admitted he would tighten his web belt, cut his hair and neaten up, in other words crawl to the lifers, to achieve the birds of a Specialist Four and the few extra dollars a month that came with it. He was familiar with poverty, he said, and told a story. The story was of Claire, a woman he was crazy about, and the time the only gift he could afford to give her was a candy whistle. So she played tunes on the whistle all day and at the end of the day she ate it. It was a perfect gift and a perfect story.

It seemed tragic a man with such a story could be forced

into military conformity for a few extra bucks a month. He didn't even resemble the sardonic guitar player once he cleaned himself up. It wasn't long before he was ripping worn PFC stripes off his sleeves and sewing on new birds. Trimble counseled patience. Before too long, Smythe missed his next haircut. His combat boots lost their waxy gleam. The heavy .45 slipped back to its fast-draw angle. He stopped having his fatigues ironed. The lifers didn't take back his birds, and his squad mates breathed a sigh of relief.

Waiting Room Moment

WHAT HAPPENS TO time spent in the waiting rooms of your life? There must be some learned equation to explain cosmic forces that bend time spent waiting, like refractions through a dirty prism. Windows of this Germany train station are opaque with coal dust from old-fashioned steam locomotives. The loudspeaker mutters unintelligible German; a sinister, guttural sound like something from a war movie about Nazis.

One man waiting on the hard wooden seats picks his nose. A fat woman near him reads a funny paper. It always seems to be raining in Germany. Those foot-long black umbrellas that snap to full-size like a Nazi paratrooper's switchblade are a fixture; peeping out of coat pockets or tucked into inevitable *schnitzel* bags, a kind of briefcase in which blue-collar workers carry their lunch to pretend they work in a *biro*.

The waiting people have the resigned look of veteran travelers who have seen it all and don't care to see it again. Only a young blonde woman seems to vibrate with impatient anticipation of some unknown destiny. A smattering of young lovers are lost in each other, not spiritually present in the drab chilly room.

Those whose mission in life is to suspiciously observe humanity's ebb and flow all stand out on the echoing concourse between the passengers and the trains. Their dark raincoats are damp and their blank faces show calm certainty somebody here is up to something illegal or immoral, No seats out there; that kind of observer doesn't sit anyway, not German ones. Veteran

43

travelers, like infantrymen, sit every chance they get because they don't know when they will get another.

A gray-haired old woman in a dirty raincoat suddenly sits erect and begins to speak loudly to the thin air in front of her. Faces turn toward her, shocked, angry; as if someone dropped a tin tray of noisy dishes in the cathedral of their private thoughts. She ignores their reaction. She acts drunk, speaking in a loud sing-song cadence as if quoting something, or at least fashioning well-rounded phrases. A few passengers listen briefly and laugh uneasily. Most shrink in upon themselves even more and pretend she isn't there and that the waiting silence has not been violated.

She has an interesting, much-traveled face. Her incomprehensible words are colored with evident emotion and irony. It is a lonely and almost physical ache to know what she is saying. It could be something deathless that should not be lost. She climbs out of her seat and goes over to shake a traveler by his shoulder to impress a significant point, waving a finger in his startled face. He forces a smile and murmurs something under his breath. She stands over him and listens, combing her matted hair with exaggerated gestures of the fingers of both hands. Then she coughs, looks away, and begins to sing softly in a voice that sounds infinitely sad.

The loudspeaker mutters over her. Its summons reduces the crowd by a dozen or so, moving quickly as if glad to escape this waiting-room apparition. Her shoulders slump. She returns to her seat, and silence. Somewhere out in the raining night the whistle of a departing steam engine hoots forlornly. No one else speaks.

Trying to Leave Paris

SITUATION NORMAL—All Fucked Up. Here we go again. The inefficiency of the Army's attempts to evacuate France under DeGaulle's edict have once again conspired to leave me stranded in Paris, with my cash running low. They checked me out of the transit hotel and had me cooling my heels all day until they finally concluded they could not shoehorn me onto today's flight stateside.

I wound up pre-processing for another flight tomorrow and wondered if I would be sleeping on a park bench with winos and their fifty-centime bottles of skull-thumper. But the Army found me a room in the Hotel de Paris—one of many Hotels de Paris. This one is at 51, Avenue Du Maine, a two-star establishment with clean rooms and private baths.

The salon is spacious with couches and chairs and an *escritoire* done up in red and black leatherette beneath a quaint bronze chandelier. The hunting prints on the wall include riders and Walker hounds baying a European elk; and a scatter-gunner concealed beside a marsh with a pointer and a setter. A wide picture window opens onto the tree-lined boulevard, beyond which a massive multi-story building is being constructed.

Paris seems to be building everywhere—building upward, above the old low skyline. Jackhammers and rivet guns and rumbling cement and gravel trucks form cacophonous counterpoint to the incessant bleat of taxi horns and click of high heels. The fresh raw odor of new construction blends with old stale ozone from Metro gratings. Paris roars and thunders and beeps and clops and laughs and propositions twenty-four hours a day.

I stood in the doorway with the *petite chien* belonging to the *proprietaire* to watch *le passage des pietons*: bearded students, *chic* women and *hommes serieux* in tailored business suits with the self-important comportment of men involved in building and running this new Paris.

Then there are the whores, icons of old Paris. I am developing a special fondness for these. Down here in Mont Parnasse they go to work early, 1600 hours, and shout their wares like fishwives to the serious men. These are not as slender, well-built and lovely as the ones assigned to patrol the *Etoile* for tourists. But they compensate with sheer Renaissance size, proportion and laughing enthusiasm.

If I had known the Army would screw things up as usual today I would have got a phone number from the little blonde who invited me to breakfast this morning. But I didn't. And I am too low on funds to consider a farewell fuck with one of these...

Scribbles on Hotel Stationery 1966

WHEN I CHECKED into the upscale Olympic Hotel in Seattle I showed them my military ID card, which garnered me a deep discount off a very nice room and no smarmy attitude from the desk clerk. The knowledgeable lifers at Fort Lewis tipped me off to the perk. I was still surprised when it worked the way they said, after my negative experiences in Tacoma. Tacoma is a GI town, my sergeant said, that's why; they're all in business to fleece us, not respect us. Get the hell away from Tacoma if you want to enjoy a three-day pass.

He gave me this advice after I made the mistake of trying to rent a car in Tacoma while in uniform. The rental agent sneered and pointed to a newspaper page pinned to the office wall: a photo of a twisted car wreck. A necklace of beer-can pop tops had been strung together to hang from the same pin, together with a hand-lettered sign: "this is why we don't rent to GIs."

In Tacoma, wearing an Army uniform makes you an instant nigger.

Which is why I was reluctant to ask for the GI discount in Seattle, the military ID giving the lie to my button-down Enro and Cricketeer tweed sport coat. But I got the red-carpet treatment, as if being a soldier here was something worth respect: go figure.

Emboldened, I called Avis from the courtesy phone in the Olympic lobby. The first thing they wanted to know was what credit card I had. Everybody in the world is beginning to want a credit card: American Express or Diners Club.

The only guy I ever knew who had one of these cards was an MP in Germany who was successful in business before his draft number came up. He told me about it after German employees of American Express at Landstuhl refused to honor my letter of introduction from the Jacksonville Beach Bank president, identifying me as a substantial account holder and guaranteeing my checks.

Letters of introduction is the way things were done in the old days, my businessman-turned-MP buddy told me; you need to get one of these; and showed me the green plastic card.

But I didn't. Back in the U.S., I figured my bank letter should suffice. No, the Avis clerk said politely, a letter doesn't constitute a "piece of ID." Without a credit card, you need two pieces of ID, one of which is your driver's license. It would be helpful if one piece had your photo on it.

I had two thoughts: one, based on my Tacoma paranoia, was that he was fishing for me to admit being a GI. My military ID was the only thing I'd ever seen with a photo on it. I didn't want to show it and risk rejection again. My second thought: totalitarian America is coming on faster than I thought. In *Sleeping Planet,* the alien empire opposing humanity required photo ID of all its subjects, movement-control permits, constant surveillance—a science-fiction version of the Third Reich blended with elements of the Soviet Union and stirred together with technology designed to ensure total population control. I made it a plot point that my human heroes would rather die fighting than knuckle under to such crap.

Within two years of my book's publication, minus conquest by either aliens or the Soviet Union, I need two "pieces of ID" (it would be helpful if one had a photo) to rent a damn car!

I almost said screw it and gave up on wheels for my three-day holiday from the Army. Then inspiration struck. The smartest thing I ever did was hang onto the Jacksonville *Journal* press card that Elvin Henson, the managing editor, handed me the day Dick Bussard, city editor, witnessed my signature on the Doubleday contract for hardback publication. A genuine press card still intimidates people.

Taken together with my Florida driver's license, which requires you to list your occupation (reporter), Avis sent someone immediately to the hotel to pick me up and gave me a sparkling new yellow Dodge Polara, black leather interior, plenty of pep. Can you spell obsequious? (Must be a big story to bring you all the way from Florida, the Avis guy said. Too big to talk about, I said.)

With a fast car and time on my hands I decided to temporarily stay ahead of Earl in terms of foreign countries visited. As soon as *Kearsarge* leaves Yankee Station for liberty in Subic Bay, he will tie me again. I headed for Vancouver, straight up Interstate Five to the border, then King George Highway north of the line; no perceptible change to the pavement.

I strolled around a bit, put gas in the Polara. (They measure it in liters and gave me Canadian change for my American dollars. Buying gas by approximately the quart seemed pretty strange.)

I found The Oyster Bar on Granville Street, which offered up the best and freshest fried shrimp I have ever tasted since that place on pilings alongside the Edisto River, South Carolina, where the shrimpers unloaded right behind the restaurant. For some reason Granville Street reminded me of the Hauptstrasse in Heidelberg, where I feasted on venison at Perkeo's.

I basically just walked around a while, letting the food settle, smiling at all the pretty Canadian girls, then headed back to Seattle. When I get back to the fort, they will ask me how drunk I got. When I tell them I had only one after-dinner drink in Vancouver, they will ask me which whore fished me for all my money, and was she worth it? When I say no whores this trip, they will be wondering what the hell I did. I guess I throw away money differently than these other soldiers.

Not sure they would get it if I said I spent my money pretending I am a civilian for a couple of days, entitled to all those automatic privileges and courtesies to which a civilian (especially one with a press card) is automatically entitled. It's as good as suddenly being promoted to colonel.

Headshrinkers can make what they will of my pathological desire to "pass for white," so to speak and hide the fact that I am (spit out the word like a Tacoma car rental agent) a *GI*.

Fetterman

QUIET WEEKEND in the old Second World War barracks that houses the headquarters platoon of Fort Lewis Training Center. I sit alone on my bunk writing, and look up and down the twin rows of double bunks and lockers, each representing a man and his individual dreams.

For some reason I think of Fetterman the Unclean. Fetterman was not his name but it will do. In Fontainebleau, our headquarters platoon at Caserne Larisboisiere considered him a half-moron. What do you call a Fetterman with an IQ of 100? His entire family going back to his grandparents. A tired old joke originally directed at Mexicans, resurrected for Fetterman.

Fetterman the Unclean was a clerk, scrawny and ugly, who seldom bathed, hence his nickname. His face was constantly red in some kind of unseemly rash, and constantly infested with erupting pimples that a little judicious soap and water might have cleansed. Every time he shaved, that awful redness was severely inflamed and being a soldier he had to shave his sparse whiskers daily. His beaked nose shone like Rudolph's, right along with his burning cheeks. His entire reading consisted of those women's magazines like *True Confessions*, which he absorbed with rapt attention. Where he found them on an Army post we had no idea.

Fetterman spent his money like water at the Enlisted Men's Club on two-bit female singers who came through in a steady rotation, and never got a tumble. But they always seemed content to permit him to buy all their drinks until he ran out of cash and they dumped him, which made him a source of contempt to other GIs.

When I worked late in headquarters on the garrison newspaper, writing stories or developing film, he was almost always duty driver for the duty officer. I remember him sitting in the disheveled duty driver's bunk in the next office, watching me work without comment. They always had to air the room out next morning. He bought the duty-driver assignment from others who hated it because he always needed money.

He seemed to ache to be a big-shot, and was routinely harassed by just about everybody. He was always catching hell—and a lot of times he deserved it for bone-headed things he did. When DeGaulle ordered NATO out of France and the evacuation began, a loudmouth from Texas tore up Fetterman's orders for rotation home and threw them away when he left them on his bunk to go to the latrine. The others told him he wouldn't be able to leave France now. It sent Fetterman into wholesale panic. It must have taken all the courage he possessed to go back to Processing and ask for a duplicate set.

Looking at rows of lockers now at Fort Lewis, one for uniforms and one for civilian clothes for each soldier, I remember the single lockers in France and how dismally empty Fetterman's was when he opened it to pack. Besides his uniforms there were two or three civilian shirts and pairs of pants, all exuding the musty odor of unwashed Fetterman into the squad bay. After he packed his duffel bag, everything besides his Army issue fitted a small AWOL bag including a couple of confession magazines.

I got my own orders shipping me across the world to Fort Lewis, with a week's annual leave in Paris before my flight. Fetterman dropped entirely out of my awareness. Somehow he must have wound up on the same chartered 707 as me, but every seat was filled with returning soldiers and dependents and I never saw him. I still wonder why the frantic swirl of arriving plane loads of troops at McGuire Air Force Base, New Jersey, washed me into a quiet backwater of activity for a strange moment—and showed me Fetterman one last time.

He was standing in the embrace of his mother and girlfriend, his mottled face so happy he did not even look like ugly Fetterman the laughing stock. His girlfriend was damn cute. She gazed up at him the way men dream of women looking at them. His short, small-framed father, whose stooped posture somehow signaled perpetual underdog, stood by with pride suffusing his features.

When Fetterman spoke to them, his voice was choked with emotion:

"Let's get the hell out of here. Let's go home."

His father led, carrying the duffel and AWOL bag. Fetterman disappeared into the thronging uniforms with his arms around his mom and his girlfriend. Now, sitting here on a quiet Army afternoon with the empty bunks and closed lockers, each representing a man who is number one in the story of his own life, Fetterman's triumphant homecoming is what I remember.

Deux Rochelles

WORKINGS OF MEMORY are a mystery. When I woke up today I was thinking of the word Rochelle. Just that: Rochelle, a French town. Quickly followed by New Rochelle, in New York State. I had thought of neither for years, yet here they were, linked as always by a decision of the imperious Charles DeGaulle.

Monsieur Chaigneau's craggy, distinguished features swam into my mind's eye. He was the only native of Rochelle I ever knew; dead loyal to DeGaulle but appalled at his politics. We shared an office at an American garrison outside Paris the spring President DeGaulle kicked NATO out of France. I had transferred from the MPs and come down from Germany to edit the garrison newspaper; M. Chaigneau was the post's community liaison.

Next a second, less-distinguished, callow and New York sort of face came next to mind; the only resident of *New* Rochelle I ever knew. I'll call him Dow. The two Rochelles – deux Rochelles – always are connected if I think of them at all.

M. Chaigneau was dismayed at tension between old allies. He attempted futilely to smooth things over by organizing Franco-American cultural events that were attended only by West German and British NATO officers; the French military gave them a pass because DeGaulle had informants in every battalion. M. Chaigneau stood to lose his livelihood when NATO left and would find it difficult finding work as a former employee of the Americans. He shrugged eloquently; nothing would be as bad as life under the Nazis. His stories of near starvation and survival in Rochelle under Nazi occupation were stark.

Dow was an American GI with his own bone to pick with DeGaulle. I met Dow when we both washed up at North Fort Lewis, Washington, exiles to the other side of the world from the City of Light. North Fort was a ghost town: abandoned temporary barracks from the Second World War stretched, empty and lightless, for miles. Huge wooden mockups of troop transports, still wreathed in rotting embarkation nets, showed where soldiers practiced for MacArthur's island-hopping campaign against the Japanese. Civilian contractors swarmed the barracks, preparing them to serve one more conflict; Vietnam. The plumbing didn't even work. The trick was to take a roll of toilet paper, find a toilet not yet used by another GI, do your business and leave it for the contractors to clean up.

One small cluster of barracks had been provided lights and running water and a mess hall but they hadn't got around to toilets even there. There was not an officer to be seen.We were roughing it the Army way until things were up and running. Senior non-coms liked this just fine; officers would only slow things down. And being assigned as cadre meant their odds were good to avoid Southeast Asia for at least another tour, maybe long enough to retire.

For amenities we had the main fort, fully operational and crammed with Fourth Division soldiers, a short bus ride away. Theaters, PXs, Class 6 Stores, snack bars and doughnut shops; everything a small town had. But that wasn't enough for Dow. His previous billet had been heaven: clerking in an Army office in Paris and *required* to wear civvies, to avoid offending French sensibilities. The Army rented a Paris flat for his squad; no barracks for him. In the jargon of the day, he had it knocked—until he didn't.

The ghostly North Fort was a long way to fall from Paris. We swapped Paris stories as an antidote for the grim surroundings. Dow was fascinated that M. Chaigneau took on Doris Lessing's *The Golden Notebook* to translate. A Lessing fan who spoke French, Dow wondered if the old man could pull off such a difficult feat. M. Chaigneau had been impressed that I remembered French Rochelle as the scene of a rollicking adventure in *The Three Musketeers*. Dow thought every literate person must know that.

But transition from life on the boulevards to baggy fatigues in a fort without plumbing preyed on Dow. More than once he said he was going over the hill. More than once he said he was losing his mind. His harping on mental illness led me to tell him the Army legend about a soldier always searching for a particular piece of paper. The legend goes the soldier one day started picking up and examining each piece of paper he came across. He would shake his head sadly, say "that's not it," and move on. He did this day in and day out. His sergeant worried about his obsession. His captain worried. But he kept on examining every piece of paper, even trash during police call. "I'll know it when I see it," was all he would say.

So they sent him to an Army shrink. He examined every piece of paper the shrink let him touch: "that's not it." The legend is vague how the shrink tried to plumb his obsession. He never stopped searching. Eventually the Army concluded he was unfit for duty and gave him a medical discharge.

"That's it," he said when they gave him his discharge.

Dow laughed at the story, but lapsed back into melancholy. Days went by. Little by little the cadre got North Fort up and running. Regular assignments replaced cleanup details. The first recruits arrived for processing. I lost track of Dow and thought no more about him. I was editing the North Fort news out of a former dispensary when I heard about a GI who had been AWOL for a year and showed up at headquarters in the middle of the night. He was dressed in European clothing and had hippie-long hair. This apparition told the astonished duty officer he had to find his father right away—and named our general as his father.

Told the general didn't have a son his age, he confessed he had memory issues—couldn't remember where he had been lately. But Dad would fix it. The MPs came and took him to the mental ward. Eventually somebody ran his fingerprints and discovered he was AWOL. He calmly denied his identity and kept asking for his father, the general. Dad would straighten it all out. He was tractable and friendly even when they put in him new fatigues and escorted him to a military barber who nearly scalped him. He just kept asking for his dad and smiling peacefully. Drug screens were negative.

Our major, the commanding general's public information officer, just shook his head. The kid was so plausible he said, some senior staff secretly wondered about the general's earlier life. The better part of valor was to issue the freshly shorn soldier a medical discharge and ship him home to New Rochelle without comment.

New Rochelle, New York? Do you know any others, my major asked. Just the original Rochelle in France, I said. A couple days later, in the brand-new North Fort snack bar, somebody hailed me from across the room. It was Dow with a fresh crew cut, neatly dressed in civvies, lugging an AWOL bag. He said he was waiting for the bus to take him to the airport. We both ordered burgers and Cokes and chatted about nothing in particular. He said he was going back to Paris soon. We exchanged addresses, finished our burgers and sipped our Cokes.

"Finally out of the Army, huh?" I said.

"I got an early discharge," he said. "Thanks to you."

"What?" I didn't think I could have heard him right.

"Remember the soldier always looking for a piece of paper?"

"Well sure." I suddenly had a very bad feeling.

He laughed happily. "I elaborated on your theme." Then he leaned in and very quietly told me he thought amnesia and paternity were more elegant, because he didn't have to stay on-post to pull it off. He unzipped his AWOL bag and produced his discharge papers.

"Story has the same punch line," he said with a skunk-eating grin. He waved the discharge. "That's it!"

Philosophy of the Graves Registrar

THE YEAR WAS 1966, the place was Fort Lewis, Washington, and a lot of uniformed young men were passing through on their way to that small hot insect-ridden hostile country in Southeast Asia.

For reasons forgotten, a GI from Detroit, last name Garcia, came through the office that day—maybe to complete a hometown news release. He was assigned to work in Graves Registry over there, counting up and registering the bodies of losers in the jungle war games who would come home in body bags. A grisly duty, but he said it was at least better than line infantry.

A very opinionated young man, Garcia was, fresh from an automobile assembly line where he made $3.80 an hour. He announced to all and sundry that he was utterly opposed to the taking of human life.

"But I like the firepower of that M-16," he added. "Because it will just flat blow them away in a hail of bullets."

Somewhat contradictory statements, someone in the office observed drily.

"Hey – I got my job on the assembly line guaranteed when I get back, and I got my brand-new car – and my girlfriend!" He thought for a moment. "What do they have to live for? Nothing! Rice? Nothing! Better they should die than me."

The GI's Tale

WE HERE IN THE STATESIDE Army this Vietnam era have been reduced all the way back to Chaucer, sitting on drawn-up foot lockers in a rough circle, as before a fire in an ancient inn, passing an illicit jug of Irish whiskey from hand to hand and each of us in turn telling his tale.

Some of them accuse me of trying out story plots and dialogue on them for my writing, under the guise of recounting actual experiences. I.Z. who knows me a little better than the rest, says I just rearrange the truth for more dramatic impact and try to read all sorts of things not actually present into situations we have been in.

I think he still is smarting some, because I read the Portland whore correctly and he did not. He waved at her through a restaurant window and she immediately jumped up and ran out of the restaurant to ask where he knew her from. He suavely said he didn't know her, but would like to. She smiled and joined us without further ado in our walk through the cold rain. She asked him where he worked and he said you don't want to know, a conditioned response for draftees in the flower-child years. He asked her where she worked and she ducked her head and said you don't want to know, which he found charming.

They were hitting it off well as he leaned solicitously toward her short curvy figure. He was like some avuncular caricature in his trademark shades on a dark winter night, wearing his white London Fog raincoat and New England penny loafers. I drew him aside and said I would leave them to it, don't let her fish you. He thought I was wrong. But I wasn't. He solved his embarrassment at being wrong in his inimitable way: he screwed her on my bed in the double room we rented for our three-day pass. So whenever you tell *this* one, he said with an evil grin, I can always top it: you came in too drunk to notice and went right to sleep in it.

Two-Fisted Irishman

WE WERE VERY YOUNG in those days and convinced we were the star of any story into which we stumbled. But it was hard to ignore that everyone else was living their own epic, in which we were bit players. A two-fisted Irishman proved that sometimes the best we could aspire to in those parallel odysseys was the role of sidekick.

I.Z. and I considered Specialist Four Gerald Murphy a bit player in our own stories. A mild-mannered young man from the Midwest with an Irish name, a cowlick that defied Army regulations and front teeth pushed sideways, he alleged, in teenage brawls. He was small and wiry compared to us. The Army had designated him unit clerk-typist, and with the unconscious arrogance of large men we more or less discounted his pugilistic tales.

The best place for a three-day pass back then was Portland, Oregon, well south of and across the vast Columbia River from military installations. None of us wanted to be taken for a GI by the girls in that free-love hippie era. The three of us enjoyed the first day of our pass with sumptuous meals followed by an extensive pub-crawl. There were marvelous bars, from the Embers with its Go-Go dancers and pool tables, to a Casbah-themed joint that featured serving girls in filmy harem attire, to a weird place full of outlaw bikers and other hard-cases that played Joan Baez exclusively on the jukebox while a virginal blonde in pale blue pinafore and petticoats, who looked as if she might have stepped out of *The Sound of Music,* served the animals.

We lost Gerald in the Casbah. He never did see the Von Trapp blonde because we could never find the place again. I. Z. reckoned it had been like Brigadoon. Gerald reckoned we had been too drunk to find it again. But that discussion came the third night. At the end of the first night, we were already sleeping off our whiskey and wondering where Gerald was when we heard the key scraping in the door of our suite, and muted cursing. We got up and let him in. He was half-laughing and all drunk and the knuckles on both his hands were skinned. We put on our shades because the light hurt our eyes and sat up in bed. There had to be a story. And there was.

Did we remember the hot older woman he was dancing with at the Casbah? We did. Right after we left, he said, some obnoxious asshole came out of the dark and punched him and yanked at the woman in his arms. What did Gerald do? He held up his left hand. "I knocked him cold. One punch."

I.Z. and I looked at each other. "Cops?" I said.

"Nah." He was chuckling, his gaze turned inward. "She dragged me out of there and drove me to her place and fucked my brains out."

We looked at each other again. He got in a fight--and got lucky too? It sure looked like he was the main character in this Portland story. But I.Z. kept his eye on the ball: "So how did you skin your right hand?"

His chuckle became an outright laugh. "I was naked as a jaybird, walking to the bathroom, when somebody jumped me in the hall."

"In her house?" I said.

"Yep." He held up his right hand. "Straight overhand right. I used a left hook in the bar."

"*Another* fight?"

He snorted. "No *fight*. I cold-cocked him too."

"What happened next?" I.Z. said.

"Man, she was all over me right on the carpet. I didn't think I could go again, but damn! She was hot as a two-dollar pistol." He was chuckling like that demented cartoon woodpecker. We shut up and listened; no way could he end the story there. And he didn't. "When she was through with me I didn't think I could get up but she said I had to, and get dressed, and leave. I couldn't just keep knocking her husband out. He might get a concussion. She called a cab and gave me cab-fare because she lived way out in the suburbs. He was still out when I left."

"Husband," I said.

"Yep. Said she never had better sex in her life and if she could get loose she'd meet me tonight back at that place."

He was exhausted and no damn wonder. He trundled off to his room. We turned off the light, put our shades away and went back to sleep. On I.Z.'s worldly advice we had gin-and-tonics with breakfast to chase hangovers and lounged around watching weekend TV football until dusk.

By mutual consent, we then accompanied Gerald back to the Casbah. Her husband might be lurking. Or the cops. But the cute bartender told us they brought the unconscious man around and sent him home in a taxi and did not inform the authorities, so not to worry. We hung around a while but things seemed calm. Gerald was by now sitting with one of the best-looking harem girls--and holding hands for god's sake. Their heads were together and they were whispering and smiling. So we wandered off into the night to find our own adventure to star in. We didn't. When the bars closed we went back to the hotel.

No Gerald. Sure enough, we hadn't been asleep long when the whole key-scraping, string-of-cursing scene was repeated. We got our shades, turned on the light and let him in. This time he was unhappy. It took a while for the new tale to unfold, but fairly soon we learned it involved another one-punch knockout.

"Gerald, you're drunk," I.Z. said. "That was last night."

"Uh-uh," he said sadly. "This was tonight. They told me I couldn't keep knocking customers out every night or they would have to refuse to serve me."

Oh brother. The sad tale unwound by fits and starts. Gerald was in love with the harem girl. Forget the red-hot mama of the previous night. This was the real deal. They had talked for hours between her customers. She was a university student studying drafting. He told her he was a truck dispatcher on holiday. Bar management liked Gerald and approved of young love in bloom. I.Z. and I looked at each other: yeah, right. Gerald caught the look and insisted it was true.

So what happened this time? A customer who turned out to be one of the harem girl's regulars came over and complained to her that he felt ignored when he had cash burning a hole in his pocket for one of her trademark blow jobs.

"So you knocked him cold," I said.

No, no, Gerald said – he simply told the guy he was mistaken, this was a nice girl. But the asshole raised his voice and said she was a whore who had done half the customers there, and began listing her specialties. *Then* Gerald knocked him out.

"I wanted to hit him a lot," Gerald said darkly. "But I guess I hit him too hard the first time." He showed us his right hand – knuckles freshly scraped. Somebody's teeth might be gathering sawdust back in the bar.

His new true love jumped up, hugged his neck fiercely, brushed a kiss across his lips – then backed away and ran into the hidden rear precincts. Gerald started after her. The bouncer – a guy as big as us – stepped to intervene – but the manager waved him off.

"Good thing for the bouncer," I.Z. muttered.

"So how did it end *this* time?" I said.

Poor Gerald. The manager said he would ask her to come out and talk to him if he would lay off the fisticuffs. But she wouldn't come out. The manager swore he tried to convince her, but she was back there crying her eyes out. Gerald just didn't understand. The manager called over the female bartender and said *you* tell him, guy like Gerald won't hit a woman. So she put her arm around him and told him: the harem girl really dug him and had not wanted him to know she turned tricks. Gerald said then we're even: I didn't want her to know I was a soldier. I'll tell her that, the bartender said and went in the back. But it was still no go. That's when the manager told him he had to quit knocking customers out or they would have to blackball him. Gerald didn't know what to do, so he just left.

It was a long time before we could get him to bed. He may never have slept. We tried to picture an establishment that ran whores showing that much tender regard for a lonesome Irishman and couldn't quite figure it out. We always thought hoodlums and hookers with hearts of gold were fiction. Our world view was upended, not least because we had been turned into sidekicks for this particular hero's odyssey. But sidekicks have their roles. The following evening we donned our white trench coats and shades and marched on the Casbah without Gerald. We left him drinking like an Irishman in another bar. He wasn't afraid to go back, but his heart was broken.

Our plan was simple: we would insert our 6'2 near-200-pound bulks shoulder-to-shoulder. We would tell the establishment our Chicago boss heard his son Gerald got in a scrape over a woman and the woman was afraid she was in trouble. We were there to be sure anyone causing trouble for a woman favored by the boss's son knew trouble flowed both ways. I swapped cash at the hotel for a roll of quarters to curl into my fist, an old juvenile delinquent trick in case the bouncer got obnoxious.

No role-playing was necessary. The female bartender recognized us right off as Gerald's friends, and with that almost telepathic sense of good bartenders knew we were there on a mission. Gerald's girl isn't here, she said. She quit last night, the bar *and* tricks. But she was afraid to ever face him again. No she would not tell us where his girl was. Yes she would give her a message. We were due to leave in the morning. Best we could do was our Army phone number, Gerald's last name and our Army mailing address. So much for being successful sidekicks.

We found Gerald and told him the bad news, got drunk on Irish whiskey for solidarity and poured ourselves on a northbound Greyhound the next morning. Gerald wouldn't talk about her. We didn't push. He never said if she wrote or called. Within two months he took a day off from clerking to qualify with the new M-16, a requirement for going to Viet Nam, and revealed he had a port call in Oakland for a combat engineer's battalion. And that's the last I saw of the two-fisted Irishman.

Farewell Clop

I.Z. SAID IT WOULD be hard to find a decent weekend clop in a city as "where-yuz-from" as Tacoma. But we decided to give it a try, since his time at Fort Lewis was running out. It would be our farewell clop. He said wryly that he was packing his peculiar vocabulary with his uniforms for transfer to Vietnam. "Where-yuz-from" was his slang for a nowhere place. The first thing kids hanging around corner stores in Philadelphia with nothing to do said to a stranger. "Clop" was his term for adventure, based on the opening scene in an early TV detective series, *Boston Blackie*, in which an anonymous man in a trench coat walked rapidly through a night city, heels ringing on the cobblestones.

So we donned our Hollywood shades and our white clop-coats and headed for Tacoma. His was a genuine London Fog raincoat that he always folded carefully in restaurants, label out, and mine was a knockoff from a PX in Germany. Both of us stood 6'2 and weighed right at 200 pounds in those long-gone days and resembled big Bobbsey Twins in our look-alike outfits. Katzenjeimer Kids was more like it.

When we got to the Tacoma Greyhound Station, he spotted some sleazy-looking kids hanging around the entrance and told me they were looking to score some dope. I would have given them a pass, but not Ivars. He marched right up to them and in his best Latvian-Pennsylvania Dutch growl wanted to know where the action was. The kids said they'd show us. Against my better judgment we wound up in the back seat of one of their tarted-up cars driving to some suburban neighborhood, where beneath a couple of street lights another gang of young hoods waited tensely, their faces lost in shadow.

"What the hell is this?" I.Z. growled. But I knew: it was a rumble waiting to happen.

Our hosts piled out and squared up. I didn't want to get out of the car, but I.Z. was out before I could say anything, striding toward the opposing force, clop coat swishing around his long legs, laughing insanely.

"Where are the girls?" he demanded roughly. "Dammit, we're looking for girls."

Oh brother. I got out of the car and stood with my hands in my coat pockets. Maybe they would think I was armed. I heard the kids ask if he had dope. I heard the scorn in his reply. Our hosts shifted nervously, looking between the other gang and his face-shoving act. I couldn't hear everything. But abruptly the other kids were dispersing, getting into parked cars, leaving. I.Z. marched back, got in the car like a commanding general, and said, "Shit, that was a waste of time. Let's go find some girls."

These kids were not accustomed to being pushed around; they were sullen. I still expected trouble. But they didn't know how to deal with his bald contempt. We wound up back at the bus station and they were glad to be rid of us. "Losers," I.Z. said. "Perfect for this where-yuz-from town. "When you put this in your damned notebook put it under 'Clop for a Lost Weekend.' Let's get a drink."

We got several. The night crawled by and they kicked us and everybody out at closing time. We nearly picked up two women who were leaving a cabaret across the street by asking for a lift. They said they had to drive up the street to turn around, and must have come to their senses and kept right on going. We took a local hotel room to sleep it off and woke up in time to watch a televised basketball game he wanted to see, between the 76ers and the Knicks. By then I was hungry enough to risk my unsettled stomach and I.Z. had a headache, so we found a buffet in walking distance and ate a lot. The little waitress who had our table poured us over ten cups of coffee apiece, which was just right for the two hours we sat there recovering. He was in a contemplative mood, and began to tell a little of his life history.

He was born in Riga when Latvia was occupied by Nazi armies. The Soviets counterattacked while he was barely old enough to walk. Many citizens of Riga—including his parents—chose the Reich over the USSR. They fled toward Berlin. He had a fragmentary memory of a bridge across some river, his mother running with him in her arms, while overhead the Soviet air came down to strafe and bomb.

His first cohesive memories were of air-raid alarms in the night, bombs raining down on Berlin, urgent whispers of the grownups about crumbling German armies in the east and west. Russians and Americans were coming, advancing on their final objective, Berlin. They may have prayed for the Americans to win the race, among terrifying concussions from bombs, explosion after explosion, debris showering down. He remembered daytime vistas of lifeless ruins everywhere. In the shadow-land of his memory Berlin was uniformly gray and sterile and dead.

He said the family photo albums were full of pre-war

and early-war shots: him and his playmates standing among smiling military men in crisp German uniforms. Neighbors, he said, home on leave from France, from Africa, from the Russian Front. One by one, they stopped coming home. All families have stories about their children, told and retold into something like legend: the family story about I.Z. is that as a tiny toddler he marched up the first American infantry he saw in the street, soberly executed a classic Nazi salute and said, "Heil Hitler!"

The Americans placed his family in a DP camp in Wurzburg. Eventually they were sent to Pennsylvania for resettlement since they couldn't go home again. His parents had run their own clothing store in Riga, attended Paris fashion shows and been fairly well-to-do. The only work they were given was as field hands for Quaker farmers. He said the Quakers were harsh taskmasters. From that final dead-end they struggled into more accommodating professions—his mother selling clothes and his father riding armored cars as a shotgun guard. Now years later, his mother still working, his father had descended into the shadows of senility, and he was tagged for the 41st Artillery, scheduled for Vietnam in August. "All I hear at home is the war," he said glumly. "Now I get to see a war of my own.

Florida and Georgia Stories from Long-ago

Seaman's Log, Interrupted

A FADED GREEN hard-cover log-book the size of a paperback novel with the U.S. Navy logo incised on the cover. The first 20 numbered pages were torn out long ago. The next two are blank. Words begin on page 22, in ink from a pen with a scratchy nib.

"May 13, 1919 … U.S.N. Enlisted at Augusta Georgia and sent to Atlanta then to hampton rhode v.a. for training. Made sharpshooter at rifle range, seven months in seaman guard. Jan 27, 1920 to Feb 28 in hospital sent to unit B feb 28. To March 22 in unit B."

An entire year of naval service compressed into one paragraph that raises more questions than it answers. It is as if he didn't start writing until he spent a month in the hospital, and then summarized things when he finally went to sea. He was seventeen years old.

"March 23 draft sent to U.S.S. Proteus at Pier 2. March 25 left Pier 2 for Guantanamo Bay Cuba."

After that, terse entries: nothing of what he saw, did, felt or experienced.

March 26 at sea

March 27 at sea

March 28 at sea

March 29 sighted land. Cuba. Dropped anchor in Guantanamo Bay.

March 30 U.S.S. Lebanon came alongside for coal and water. March 31 filling water barges and unloading cargo

April 1 U.S.S. Lebanon shoved off. Coal and water.

April 2 Coal the U.S.S Culgoa. April 3 loading on stores. April 4 taking off stores. April 5 over the side. Fleet left for target practice. April 6 left for Guantanamo Bay Cuba. April 7 arrived at same. Pulled alongside Blackhawk then left her and anchored April 8. Pulled alongside Bridgeport and gave her stores oil and gasoline. Off and anchored. Tug 51 came alongside for stores. Tug 51 shoved off. Tug 40 came alongside for stores. Tug 40 shoved off.

Three p.m. left for Kingston Jamaica.

April 9 at sea 2:30 p.m. arrived at Bay and anchored. Lifted anchor underway to pier, tied up to pier Kingston Jamaica.

April 10 getting water and liberty

April 11 same

April 12 same also left Kingston Jamaica for Guantanamo Bay Cuba.

April 12 arriving at Guantanamo Bay Cuba and tied up to the U.S.S Columbia. Left her and anchored April 14.

Admiral inspection. U.S.S. Sefanion came alongside. U.S.S. Salose came alongside for water, the Sefanion shoved off.

April 15 U.S.S Prometheus came alongside for water. U.S.S Salose shoved off. Tugs 15 and 23 came alongside for water. Tugs and Prometheus shoved off and we left for Guantanamo Bay.

April 16 arriving at Guantanamo Bay Pulled alongside U.S.S. Florida gave her coal and water. Shoved off and anchored April 17 taking off gasoline and paint putting it on barges.

April 18 Pulled alongside U.S.S. N. Dakota to give her coal and water...

Intriguing glimpses into the logistics of a coal-burning Navy; his personal log shadowed the official ship's log. Some of the recorded ship's names seem unlikely at best. With only a second-grade education he was a free-style speller. His career ended with a laconic phrase: "Sent out for fighting. BCD." But the log recorded that "sent out" was only a phrase; they made him chip rust and paint do all the other chores of an able-bodied seaman the whole voyage back to Richmond, rather than cool his heels in the brig. Then they cashiered him and he went home. For a few pages he logged efforts to find work in the cotton mills in an era where work was hard to come by. Then he just stopped writing and put the book away and never picked it up again. It was found in his trunk half a century later, after he died.

The mystery of the torn-out pages is forever lost in time. Oral family history says he was discharged for nearly killing a chief petty officer with his fists after the chief called him a nigger. He married a rumrunner chieftain's girlfriend and the rumrunner held his peace. His temper and his titanic strength were well-known, and he was a dead shot. He had the nearly illiterate's incredible memory skills; his wife used her connections to bootleg a copy of the city fireman's entrance exam and he memorized the entire thing and posted a perfect score.

They had four children and raised them on a fireman's salary, and he was the driver at Old Number One house for twenty-five years. There was nothing about fighting fires he did not know and could not do. His sons fought in two wars and his daughter married two soldiers in a row, her childhood sweetheart home from the Pacific after she divorced her wartime paramour. He and his wife raised the two grandchildren. Later they looked after a son of one of his sons after a divorce, who later remembered the time with his grandfather as the best of his childhood.

That same grandson later called the fireman an American hero born and raised in violent poverty who righted himself and served with distinction as a civil servant. He was the lynchpin between cotton-mill workers and his progeny: his sons an Army general, a state politician and an Episcopal priest, his daughter a career Postal Service employee. One son and one grandson even served in the Navy without getting in trouble. His consistent advice to sons and grandsons leaving for the service, whether Army or Navy: hold your temper and don't get in any fights; you don't know your own strength. The bitter lesson from a seaman's log, interrupted.

Old Man on a Ladder

THE CHANGE in the sound of the surf woke the old man. When he opened his eyes, the room was still gloomy–dark. He could see the window and the jalousie door at the end of the small room. The window panes and the jalousie slats were dim grey smears. It was morning.

For fifteen years now the change in the sound of the surf had been his alarm clock. The big Seth Thomas on the little shelf he'd build ticked loudly in the dark, but it didn't chime anymore. It had chimed all his thirty working years for the city, but it didn't any more. The salt air got to it two years after he and the old lady had come to Florida to retire.

Now in the morning there was that other burbling, low–pitched, self–satisfied birdy sound. Those goddamn pigeons, preening and cooing and getting ready to shit all over his favorite sunning chair and the old lady's wash. Those fancy–ass Jews up on waterfront had started it by feeding them when the first pigeons wandered into the neighborhood. There hadn't been any pigeons for fifteen years until that spring, and now there were dozens of the filthy things staining his lawn furniture, the sides of the house, everything. They lived to shit, it seemed.

They had never been there when he could have handled them. But now they were. Scratching and burbling under the eaves of the house, trying to find a way into the insulation spaces. The old beach house didn't have an attic. Not many of its kind did; just space up under the roof for insulation and to crawl to get to the wiring. The pigeons wanted to get in there and he was damned if he was going to let them.

He swung his one leg from under the sheet carefully, trying to keep the bedsprings from squeaking. It was a trick he had learned on the night shifts when he didn't want to wake up the old lady coming or going. It had been pretty handy for tomming around and going fishing up the river too, all those years. That had been with two legs, though. That was before the diabetes and the amputation and Medicare. That was when he was still his own man.

The bed squeaked a little but the old lady, upstairs on the screened-in sleeping porch, was a heavier sleeper now, because it wore her out doing all the housework and waiting on him hand and foot too. His heart was beating like on his first deer hunt in the river swamps. He got his aluminum walker and sidled back to the bathroom to relieve himself. A car engine, the familiar car engine of the morning paper–route carrier, sounded in the lane. As he flushed the toilet the big Thursday edition with all the grocery specials thudded out front.

He hobbled through the kitchen and drew a cup of coffee from the pot left on simmer all night and got back to his wheel chair where it was parked at the foot of the bed. The old lady hadn't stirred. They had never slept together in forty–five years of marriage; she would come to his bed for sex and then leave again when they were done. But that had been over a long time, even before he lost the leg.

He got hold of the hand–molded plastic leg that his son who worked for the government had got him. He carefully strapped it in place and then sat in the chair and went through the routine. Heart pill, gulp of coffee; circulation pill, gulp. Then he started putting on his pants, grunting to pull the right leg over the plastic limb with its shoe on; too stubborn to unlace it. He took a short breather before putting on his sock and getting his pants all the way on and belted, and tying his other shoe.

When he was ready, he bent way over from the waist and dragged the short pellet rifle from under the bed. He braced it in the corner of the chair and rolled quietly to the door, reversed, opened the door and hitched himself out onto the concrete stoop. The rubber tires were silent as he rolled out onto the lane. It was a tarmac strip not much wider than a driveway. It had been a service entrance to the Jew–houses on ocean front. The garage apartments like his were afterthoughts, small cypress–shingle two-stories, three on each side, squatting between the oceanfront houses and First Street among dense palm and oleander trees.

He turned left and rolled at an angle toward the house across the street. Behind him, the scratching and flapping and cooing seemed to get louder. He spun the wheelchair slowly, set the brake, and took hold of the little gun.

They were on the almost flat upstairs porch roof, preening and digging for bugs. He picked out the one with the most white on it, centered the sights and squeezed the trigger. Feathers puffed as the little gun snapped. There was a sudden frantic beating of wings. He snatched the gun down, braced it and began to lever the bellows forearm, building another compression of air. He pumped eight strokes and then fumbled another of the tiny pellets into the chamber, cursing his fumbles and the gun's slowness. There was a soft thud on the tarmac. The one he'd shot had tumbled off the roof in its death throes.

One down. He hadn't forgot how to shoot. That was something he still had.

The idiot pigeons couldn't make it out. They'd had things their own way too long. They had scattered across the roof, but they hadn't flushed. He waited for his pulse to slow down and his breathing to ease. He still knew how to wait, too. That was something the deer drives and the squirrels up in those big river oaks had taught him young, how to wait. That and fishing up the river. When he got on the fire department the shift work had been good for learning to wait, too. And the swings and graveyards left him time to hunt and run a trot line on the river.

But toward the end he had got lazier about going out. The subdivisions and the paper plants ate up the swamps and crowded the river, and most of the game was gone anyway, killed by pollution or moved deeper in the swamps. Like he had moved to Florida; like he would be gone, soon. But he could still wait.

His pulse was all right now. His breathing was steady. The pigeons began to shuffle around and a couple of them burbled kind of hesitantly. One flapped off the roof to the phone wire and balanced until the wire stopped moving around. Then it complacently bombarded his deck chair by the palm tree at the corner of his lot. That one. He put the little rifle up and snapped the shot off in one movement. The bird squawked and jumped, spilling feathers, then folded up and dropped like a stone. It landed with a solid whack, not ten feet from the first one. That settled it for the others. They got out of there in a satisfying panic. He knew they would be back, though.

He had that figured out too, and if the nigger showed up now like he'd said he would, everything would be just right. It was still an hour before the old lady's little tin alarm clock would get her up to give him his insulin. Plenty of time, if Lester would just get here. Just as the old man was thinking that, he heard the clatter of a truck engine one street over. Then he didn't hear it, and then he heard a door open and close quietly.

Then Lester came up the lane, moving loose and easy in his torn sneakers. He walked with a glide – shuffle – glide, and carried his arms at a dangle like a puppet. Lester worked on the beach town's one garbage truck. He was a Georgia sharecropper who had come south six years ago to get work when his cotton failed and he had a couple run-ins with the law. He started in doing yard work around, and he'd done some for the old man.

The old man had spoken up for him when the town fathers were after a new sanitation man, because he'd got a letter from another retired fireman up in Georgia asking if he could help Lester out. The old man's recommendation got him the job. Lester wasn't young any more either but he was a rummy and one hell of a womanizer.

He and the old man were easy together. They neither one quite knew what to think about those lunch counter sit-ins and all that nonsense. They had both always been too concerned with making a living and woman–chasing on the side to think about things that other people just went on and on about. They didn't ever talk about how they didn't understand other people. That wasn't their style. They were just easy together.

The old woman said it nearly broke Lester's heart when he dropped by after laying out drunk for a week with a new woman and heard that the old man was in the hospital with a rotting leg. That was what she said. She said Lester checked by from time to time to see could he help out in the yard or anything.

When the old man saw him the first time after coming back from the hospital, Lester laughed a big happy laugh and said the old man was sure going to burn up a lot of wheelchair tires, 'cause Lester knew he wasn't going to stop chasing women. The old man had been braced up to fight sympathy from a black man. When he didn't get it, the bracing came loose all at once, and he laughed hard enough to bust stitches, and that wasn't just a saying at the time. They just didn't make niggers like that anymore, not even in Georgia, he bet.

Lester came up. "Mawnin'."

"Mawnin', Lester." He kept his voice down. "That was smart, parkin' over there like that."

Lester grinned. "I done learn lawng time uhgo 'bout easin' round when I doesn't want no female t' know what i'se upter." His soft voice carried just to the old man's ears. "Whur duh ladduh?"

"In there." He pointed a thumb at the garage behind him. "Neighbor said I could use it. I told him I was gonna git you t'check the roof for leaks."

"Ain't such uh bad ideuh, neithuh. The rainy time comin' on."

"Later," the old man said. "First things first."

"Awright, whur y' wan'it?"

"Around back. That's where they git in under the eaves.

Be quiet now, an' watch out. Dam' thing's heavy."

Lester dipped his head and eased into the gloom of the garage. He almost vanished in the darkness, with his ebony skin and drab denim jacket. The ladder's extension hardware went clunk, softly, as he lifted it. The old man felt his balls suck up. Don't let her catch me now, he prayed. Not like this. Not now. Please not now.

Lester sidled out of the garage taking short, lumpy steps under the weight of the ladder. His face was drawn tight.

"You okay?" The old man was straining forward, aching to put his wasted shoulder against that weight. Something solid. He half–raised himself.

"You sit easy!" Lester hissed. "I's strappin! Don't fuss yo–self. C'mon."

He moved across the lane and around the opposite side of the house from the old lady's breezeway without even hesitating. When he got the end of the ladder down on the dewy grass, the old man trundled up to its butt–end.

"Here." He wheeled into line, set the brake hard. "Walk it up to me." He planted his one good foot against it. "You try t' git it up by yo'self, you gonna make a racket."

"Okay." Lester lifted the top end, got it over his head and started walking in to the old man, keeping his hands high, pushing the ladder hand over hand into the air.

When he got up toe to toe with the old man his face was shining with sweat. The old man sniffed the sweetish odor of unbathed nigger and rum–sweat. Lester braced one side of the ladder and pivoted it around against the house and cranked up the extension. The rusty locks creaked loudly when they took hold, but nothing came of it.

"Good," said the old man. "Now git my hammer and

wire cutters and that screen mesh and my nails."

"I could do hit jest as good," Lester said, not looking at him. "I could."

"It's my house," the old man said stubbornly.

"Aw—right. Can I have them pigeons out front? Them's good eatin', do yuh know howter fix 'em."

"Sure," the old man said. "You can have every one I git. You done good. Take this pellet gun and put it on the front seat of my car. I'll sneak it back in later. Thanks for comin' on by, y'hear? I'll git a few more of 'em after this, and you can have 'em all. They'll get th' idea soon, though. Soon's I git this mesh put up and git a couple more of 'em."

He stood up with the dual care of age and amputation. "You better git now. If the old lady catches you here, it'll be hell Columbia."

"I better stay," Lester said. He kept shooting glances at the kitchen window. "I ain't wantin' no fine ole lady aftuh me 'cause I lef' yuh when yuh needed hep. . ."

"I don't need your goddamn help! Now git outta here before she catches you. I might need you to sneak me another favor and you can't if she's onto you."

The old man waited until he heard the distant truck door open and close again, and the engine groan to life and go rattling off, lifters slapping noisily. Then he got the roll of mesh in one pocket and the nails and cutters in the other, and stuck the hammer through his belt. He got his hands on the ladder and stepped up with his real leg on the first rung. Daylight was coming fast now. He straightened the leg and pulled himself up. He almost could feel the toes of the foot he didn't have reaching for the next rung. But the plastic leg hung heavily from its harness, unresponsive and alien.

Thirty years of climbing ladders for the city, he thought. For what? He bent over and got his shiny new leg behind the knee and bent it until the foot swung onto the lower rung. Now he was eight inches off the ground. He held on tight and climbed one more rung and then, leaning against the slant of the ladder, got his pant leg and got the plastic one up. Thirty years of climbing ladders had at least taught him that you go at your own speed. Right now, this was his speed. It hadn't been, but now it was. Step, bend, drag. Step, drag.

Now he was halfway up. The quiet, water–silvered grass looked farther down than the street had looked from the Culpepper Building with the roof burning and the wind threatening the whole business district of the city. The three – alarmer had been so hot he could feel the skin blistering under his helmet and thought he was going to die from the heat of it in his canvas turnout coat.

He stopped to let his heart quiet down. The stump of his missing leg ached horribly, and the harness dragged down on him. He had never been so aware of the thing's deadness and uselessness. It gave him a place to put the other shoe and make him look whole in church Sunday, that was all it was good for. He had to use it as a brace for the step–up with his real foot, and be careful. He was always careful on a ladder. That was how he had retired in one piece.

Even when the whole old–fashioned downtown section of the city had finally gone up that hot, blowing May before the Japs bombed Pearl Harbor the next winter, he had been careful. Engine companies from as far away as Aiken had responded, and firemen died.

Powell and Teech got it in that one. They went through

a roof they stayed on longer than they should have. They had Old Number One's main line right on the hot heart of the King Cotton Hotel, and the fire got under them in the Diamond Pawn Shop and pulled them down. Turnquest and Dunlap and Edstrom would have got it too, if the old man hadn't seen the big beam cutting down on them, leaning out toward them when the fire chewed it off at the base.

They were taking more line up the big ladder on the headquarters hook and ladder when the beam fell, and he hadn't had time to do anything but turn loose and tumble into Dunlap waist–high, and that knocked them all back half a dozen rungs before the beam smacked across the ladder and splintered, spraying hot sparks.

They all caught themselves all right. He had been hanging half off the swaying ladder, looking down on a blazing wilderness that used to be the Woolworth's when he noticed that Turnquest was upside down, hanging on like a spider and puking his guts out into the flames below. The old man had started laughing so hard he nearly fell off the ladder...

He was up now. The morning stretched around him, quiet and grey. He was at the place where the pigeons were trying to get in. From up here he could see the pink line of dawn running along the edge of the grey sea. A flock of pelicans, black on grey, swooped in perfect unison above the outside edge of the surf line. Farther out, he could see the pale smudges of a pair of shrimpers. He could even hear the quiet thump of their diesels as they hauled their nets.

He got out the wire and the cutters, moving with elaborate care. Turnquest would laugh his ass off if he read the old man had fallen off a ladder and killed himself.

Turnquest and Harrison were the only other ones from the old house still left. Cancer got Dunlap. Edstrom shot his wife for running around, and then blew his own brains out. Captain Benteen got it in a car wreck. Dancy got pneumonia fishing up the river in the rain when he was sixty–nine. Even the engine house had been pulled down and its number assigned to another house.

It was Harrison who had written the old man about Lester; Harrison had retired to Waynesboro to raise bird dogs and play country squire.

The old man had got a letter from Turnquest just the other day about their old house being torn down. He offered to mail the old man a brick from the rubble, which the old man thought was about as silly a thing as Turnquest had ever said.

Turnquest also went on about how the young firemen just weren't the same, but they still told the legends about Old Number One. About how the old man knocked out two of Lefty Halloran's teeth with one punch, just because he walked in off the street one summer bragging about how tough he was. Lefty was first baseman for the Sally League Tigers. He was on the bench for a month until his gums healed, and the manager fined him a hundred dollars for wising off to the old man in the first place, and he never got called up to a higher league.

They still told the story about how Dancy had screwed the broad up in the hose loft, and put the Sunday paper under her ass when she hollered about it being too dirty up there. When she came down she had Flash Gordon sweated onto her right cheek and Bringing Up Father sweated onto the left cheek, and of course Dancy had to make her show her butt to the others.

Sometimes the old man wished he'd never left Georgia. He could go around to the engine houses like Turnquest and listen to the old stories and how they got wilder and wilder over the years. They would know his name all right, soon as he mentioned it. That was where he really belonged. But you were supposed to retire somewhere, and he had come to Florida.

He unrolled a length of the wire mesh and leaned up tight against the ladder to fit it into place. His stump was throbbing like fire. He pulled the mesh back to him and half twisted around to get at it with the cutters. The plastic leg betrayed him. It buckled at the knee. He dropped the mesh and cutters and his palms slapped the rough wood of the ladder before he thought, steadying himself.

The mesh fell straight down, but the cutters hit the side of the ladder and bounced against the house with a loud whack. He hung there with his heart running away and felt the dizziness come up out of his belly, pushing sour bile ahead of it into the back of his throat. He hung on and pushed it back down. He pushed it down twice and then it stayed down. Then he waited on his heart. Then he started grimly back down the ladder.

It was slower than going up. He had to knock the plastic leg off the rung and then hang there half squatting with his ass sticking out, all his weight back off the ladder, while the plastic leg pendulumed to a stop. Then he had to brace that leg before he could step down. He had to guess whether it was on the rung solid, because he couldn't see past his own body. He had to trust it. He could feel the toes of the gone foot curling in his mind, reaching for the feel of the rung under the sole of his shoe. He had to trust the plastic leg to lock and hold his weight while he stepped off the upper rung with his real leg. When he finally got down he was sweating so bad that it ran in his eyes and blinded him.

He sat in his chair and used his handkerchief. When he was through it was sopping wet and the sweat was still coming. He tried to light a cigarette and broke one in half and dropped one on the grass before he got one lit. He sucked smoke deep in his lungs and blew it out, sucked it in again. He smoked it in ten long drags and threw what was left on the wet grass. Then he rolled over and grunted the cutters and the mesh up in his lap and rolled back to the foot of the ladder.

He was five rungs up when he heard the metallic shrill of the old lady's alarm clock. He froze on the ladder. The sun was a pregnant orange bulge on the edge of the world. He waited. The clock cut off in mid–shrill. He heard bed springs groan faintly. Then he heard, through the fabric of the house, the loud snap of the breezeway light switch.

He climbed another rung before he heard the slow shuffle of her slippers in the kitchen. They stopped and he knew she was turning up the heat under the coffee; she liked it scalding hot. Then they started up again and went into the bathroom. He heard her put the seat down and then he heard her urinate, a loud whirring sound. The sound trickled away into silence and the toilet flushed. The slippers shuffled out into the kitchen again. He heard her call his name softly, her voice slurred with sleep. He waited.

She called again, and then shuffled into the front room. He heard the front door open and close. She came shuffling back, and he heard the rubber band being pushed off the rolled newspaper. Then she rattled cups in the cupboard. The light in the dining room went on, throwing a bar of yellow out onto the grass. He heard her smoothing the paper out on the table, its pages crackling.

He looked up at where the pigeons were trying to get in. The first thing she heard, she would come out. She would come out and order him to come down and when he refused, she would go call the rescue squad like the doctor had told her to do if he got into a predicament. They were good boys. They were firemen from Jacksonville, assigned to the new rescue squads that fire departments operated now. They would probably respond faster than he could come down. His stump was pounding and his head felt fuzzy.

He had never been brought off a ladder in his life. They would come up his ladder and bring him off it. At least they would be firemen, and not damn cops. But could he get the mesh up before she came out and caught him and called them? He didn't think so. She would probably start up the ladder herself if he kept on hammering after she called the squad; she was as stubborn as he was. He had never been brought off a ladder. He never had. He had gone up his ladders when things were pretty bad. And he'd come back down every one of them. Sometimes he had brought other people off.

He brought Lassiter off when those windows in the Mi Ling Laundry exploded and got him in the eyes; fat Lassiter. He told Lassiter that if he so much as blinked, grinding the glass into his eyeballs, he would kick his ass clear to East Boundary. Lassiter was so afraid of him that he somehow controlled his blink reflex, and the eye doctors said later that saved his sight.

And he brought kids and old women down ladders, and

one redheaded broad in a negligee from the Richmond Hotel fire that he would never forget, whose cunt had been hotter against him than the fire, and who had pulled his head down and kissed his with her tongue when he put her down on the ground. Later, she came around to the engine house in a sexy dress and took him to lunch in his blue dress uniform at the Bon Air. Then she took him upstairs to her new room and screwed him three times before she let him out of there and took him back to the engine house. He had even brought a couple of kittens out of trees.

But nobody was going to bring him off a ladder. Especially not now. Not even another fireman. He worked his way back down the ladder. It seemed to take a lot longer this time, just the five rungs, and the stump was shooting sparks of pain straight up his back. He moved as quiet as he could, and it seemed to take a long time. The wire cutters clinked against the wheel chair as he was sitting down. The old lady heard that, and called out.

"Ode?""

"Yeah, it's me," he said.

Her chair scraped back and she shuffled toward the door.

"What you doin' out there?" She unfastened the screen door and came through. When she saw the ladder, she stopped dead.

"I'm plantin' corn," he said bitterly,

"How'd you get that ladder up there?" she said.

"Mind your own goddamn business!"

"It is my business," she said patiently. "Now, who did it?"

"I did it myself," he said.

"That Lester did it," she said. "He's the only one would go along with you on something as silly as this."

"He did not."

"That idiot Lester," she said. "He's crazy as you are. Salt an' pepper, that's what y'all are. Salt an' pepper, in just–alike shakers." She shook her head.

"Shut up, goddamn it." He tried to shout but his voice rasped instead. She walked closer. "You get that screen put up there?" She was looking up where the ladder was leaning. He was silent. "Well?" she said, still squinting upward.

"No," he said. "No, I did not get it up. Lester will have to do it."

"Okay," she said, looking at him now. "I'll tell him when he comes by on the trash truck. You ready for your insulin?"

"No," he said, "I am not ready for my insulin."

"You better take it."

"I'm not going to take it yet," he said.

"Why not? What you gonna do now?"

He took the brake off the wheelchair. The pain in the stump was already easing off. "I'm goin' up on the seawall an' smoke a cigarette," he said. "I'm gonna smoke a cigarette, and I'm gonna watch the sun come the rest of the way up."

"What you want for breakfast?" she said.

"I'll tell you when I get back." He put down the mesh and the cutters, and took the hammer out of his belt and the nails out of his pocket and put them down.

"Don't be all day," she said. "You still gotta take your insulin."

"I'll stay as long as I want to," he said, and started off.

She watched him push himself laboriously across the grass until he went around the corner out of sight. Then she went back inside to finish reading the paper and to wait for him to come back.

Steamboat
Lost in Time

THE SLENDER TAPERING varnished stick had a place of honor among my vinyl little cowboys and model airplanes and baseball gloves. It reminded me of the first time I had to dress up except to go to church. More, it stood for what to a pre-school boy was an amazing adventure: my first and only river voyage on a steamboat.

There was a signature on the orchestra conductor's baton, just like on a Louisville Slugger. The signature was Guy Lombardo's. They were selling them as souvenirs the night I heard his orchestra play as we steamed down the Savannah River and my grandfather bought me one. All I had to do was pick it up and my arm tried to copy Lombardo's conducting gestures from that glittering magical night.

Every time I heard one of the numbers they played on the living room radio I was transported instantly to that dark dining hall full of dressed-up grown people with the brightly lighted orchestra on stage. *Harbor Lights* and *Red Sails in the Sunset* were two of my favorites. Sometimes the grown people got up and danced. I remember it like yesterday but the Second World War hadn't been over more than a couple of years, so it was a long time ago.

I cannot remember the name of the riverboat because I never knew it. Things like that didn't seem important at my young age. What was important and kind of overwhelming was that it was the first time I was invited among grown-ups to see grown-up doings. I don't remember any other children there. Cigarettes sparked like fireflies in the audience. My unjaded nostrils recorded all sorts of exotic liquors on passing trays and on grown-ups' breath. I saw couples leave the dance floor to slip out on the side decks to snuggle and neck and watch the Savannah River flow by.

My grandfather had worked in the boiler room of coal-burning Navy ships in his youth but I didn't know that then. He took me below to educate me into what made a riverboat run. The images burned into my brain past all forgetting: shirtless black men, their muscles gleaming as if oiled, illuminated by the pulsing red maw into which they heaved shovel after shovel of coal. Intense heat and writhing shadows and laboring men; it made me think of Sunday school depictions of hell. Of course I did not share that with my grandfather who was not much of a church-goer.

Back at our table, once more immersed by the melodic big-band sounds of the Royal Canadians, while couples danced or sat and listened, I experienced a kind of disconnect between the well-fed, well-watered comfort of the audience and unlucky laborers below decks. But I didn't say anything about that either. No one could have heard me anyway and I did not understand what I was feeling. But I remembered.

There were four at our table including me: my grandparents and my mother. My uncles returned from war weren't there and it must have been the pause between my father leaving and my stepfather showing up. So I was very young. Only one other impression was recorded indelibly on my callow brain when the orchestra struck up Cole Porter's *Begin the Beguine*. Not that I knew who Cole Porter was. What I observed was a complex, wordless and distinctly unpleasant interaction between my grandparents. My grandmother had been enjoying her rare night out immensely, becoming a sort of social butterfly before my disbelieving eyes. My grandfather had been relaxed and smiling.

Now she stiffened perceptibly and flashed him a withering glance which he affected to ignore, concentrating on the orchestra. He was no longer smiling. Both sat rigidly through the entire number as if the whole riverboat had vanished and each was utterly alone. When the last note ended, he got up and said something about getting some air and walked away. My grandmother murmured to my mother and I heard the bitterness. It was clear her words were about grown-up stuff, not for my ears. I didn't learn the source of her bitterness for some years. But that little byplay stayed with me as clearly as firemen below shoveling coal; evidence life as a grown-up was not all dancing and smiles.

That's what I remember--and what that long-gone toy baton represented to me. The odd thing is that histories insist the last Savannah River steamboat to call at Augusta was in 1936. That's more than a decade before we had dinner and listened to Guy Lombardo and his Royal Canadians on a steamboat whose name I never knew.

I know this wasn't a dream. But my riverboat has been lost in time.

Mourning
For the Crossroads

WHEN I WAS a very young boy I understood pretty early that my grandmother spoke the language differently than other people. She was a born storyteller and her language evoked vivid images in my impressionable brain. One of the most vivid was when we heard a far-off train whistle in the night and she would intone: "The frogs lowered their croaking in the millpond and in the distance the midnight freight mourned for the crossroads."

It was understood without discussion that this sentence was rich with meaning. It was before I knew the lines were the opening of a never-published novel she had written as a teenager, and then burned when her mother refused her permission to accept an offer of purchase from a newspaper syndicate. Newspapers published novels in serial form back then. But writers were no better than harlots by my great grandmother's lights.

I knew what "moan" meant, and those distant train whistles sounded like they were in pain to me. In keeping with traditions of the Old South, I already had taken part in the solemnity of funerals and witnessed firsthand the formal, waxy stillness of the recently dead laid out in their coffins. So I knew what mourning was, too.

The bereaved sometimes made sounds like midnight freights out past East Boundary. The words confused themselves in my young brain.

Trains off across there somewhere had mourned for the crossroads my entire short life. I was sure they always would, an unchanging symbol of all that was distant and mysterious, and sometimes hurtful. My unquestioning certainty changed in a single moment out on the Savannah River levee.

My grandfather was always taking my brother and me shooting out on the levee. We would set up tin cans and empty whiskey bottles in the waste ground between the levee and the river, and stand up on the levee and shoot down. My grandfather said this prevented dangerous ricochets by the little .22 bullets. Every one of those colorful little pasteboard boxes containing fifty .22 Long Rifle shells had a printed warning on the flap: "Range one mile--Be Careful!" We always were. My grandfather was fierce about ricochets.

One day we were shooting on the levee near where the train tracks crossed on the way to the river trestle into South Carolina. My brother was six that year, finally big enough that my grandfather didn't have to help him hold his little Remington single-shot bolt action. He was getting to be a good shot fast, totally focused on the sights. I cradled my Marlin repeater in the crook of my arm and stared hard at the bottles to see where his shots hit.

Something went BLAT-T-T-T behind me so loud I almost dropped my rifle.

I spun around. Here came this huge silver streamlined monster of a locomotive rushing toward the levee crossing, pulling a long line of passenger cars.

They still had long passenger trains then. There was no smokestack, no steam.

"Wave," my grandfather said.

He took off the blue mattress-ticking engineer's hat he always wore outdoors and waved at the silver monster. Earl waved. I waved. The guy leaning out of the high side window of the locomotive, small as a toy soldier way up there, tugged off his own engineer's cap and waved back. The train horn went BLAT-T-T-T again. No mournful whistle.

Then the silver monster was gone, sweeping on toward the river, that harsh sound trailing away strangely. At that age I had no idea what a Doppler effect was. The passenger cars flashed by, blink-quick glimpses of people in the windows, as the rumble click-click of the steel wheels washed over us with the rush of air from the train's passage. The horn sounded again off across there, probably when the locomotive hit the trestle. I didn't realize I was staring after the train long after it was gone until my grandfather said something I didn't hear.

"What was that?" I said, meaning the locomotive. "What made that sound?"

"A Diesel locomotive," he said. "A brand new one. That was its horn."

"It doesn't sound right for a train," I said.

He just looked at me.

"Mama always says trains mourn for the crossroads," I said. "That one didn't mourn. It squawked!" I felt cheated somehow. More than that, I felt unsettled.

"Diesels sound different," my grandfather said. "They use a big air horn, not a steam whistle. Gonna be a lot of Diesels, from now on." He was checking to make sure Earl's rifle was unloaded. "Load your rifle," he said to me, the train already forgotten. "It's your turn to shoot." I reached into my pocket for some .22 shells. But I knew the world was never going to be the same again.

Night Bus to Dallas

THE FOUR OF US spent a lot of time on Greyhound buses in the forties and early fifties. Under the supervision of my grandmother, we never took a Trailways if we could help it. When my grandmother and mother took my brother and me to visit country relatives, we would wait in the school-bus shed on U.S. 1 for our country cousins to flag down the evening Greyhound to go home. When my grandmother led us across the South to Gene Autry's personal appearances, of course we took Greyhound. I once got to sit in the seat above the steps across from the driver and watch the highway unfold through the huge windshield. At seven or eight, that was a big deal.

A sage poet once remarked that our hometowns give us our first and sometimes only real sense of identity; in my hometown I learned an Aristotelian either-or philosophy that colored my whole life. I never questioned my grandmother's choice of overland bus any more than I questioned Gene Autry's preeminence among Hollywood's singing cowboys; Roy Rogers was a joke, not even his real name. You either rode Greyhound or you rode Trailways. You either backed Gene Autry or Roy Rogers; sometimes that led to grade-school fistfights and bloody noses. You bought your bread from Colonial Bakeries on Central Avenue or from Claussen's on Upper Broad. Your milk and ice cream came from Sancken's or from Augusta Dairy. Duke's Mayonnaise and Del Monte ketchup were the only real mayonnaise and ketchup; the entire list was long. We were a Greyhound and Gene Autry and Colonial and Sancken's and Duke's and Del Monte family.

We rode Greyhounds to Florida several times to scout for a house to buy when my grandfather retired. Before his retirement came the most ambitious Greyhound journey of all: clear from Georgia to Denver to visit one of my uncles; across the South into Texas with a night layover in Dallas when it still had streetcars. (And on that night, a surreal infestation of crickets crawled the walls around the Greyhound depot and created endless blue sparks as they crashed into streetcar wires.) They said in those days that by the time you crossed Texas by Greyhound, you were a resident.

But this is about the night bus to Dallas, late summer of 1954. That's when a Greyhound driver affirmed once and for all their heroic status in my grandmother's eyes. We were humming through the Alabama night when the brakes came on suddenly. This was not uncommon; we weren't the only people who stood on remote highways near farms to flag down a through-bus. I saw two ethereal feminine apparitions appear outside in its bright headlights, filmy nightclothes blowing in a breeze that revealed more than was concealed.

What was revealed were two deliciously curvaceous shapes, one dark-haired, the other blonde, their tresses in tumbled disarray around smooth white shoulders. Earlier that spring I had discovered my mother's stash of steamy romance novels which fired my pre-teen imagination. Now I watched in a daze as two negligee-clad females tripped up the high Greyhound steps in their bedroom slippers.

(Women called them "mules" then for reasons I never knew.) They were giggling and panting as they bought tickets. Of course they had their purses. At eleven I never had seen a woman without her purse however dressed; or in this case sort of dressed.

"Some seats toward the back," I heard the driver say.

They whispered to him like they were telling secrets and hurried by me in a wash of exotic perfumes that overloaded my senses. I felt my eleven-year-old ears burn when I realized I was eye to crotch with two panties-free females. They sat somewhere behind me. The bus got underway. More giggling, and now some male laughter and low urgent conversation. I would have sworn I heard one of the girls say Penis City.

I was seated by my grandmother who was unaffected by apparitions out of black night. "They're on the run," she muttered over the seatback to my mother. "Working girls from Phoenix City."

"You know what they're talking about?" my mother whispered.

Of course she did; I often thought there was nothing my grandmother didn't know. "Fleshpots for GIs," she said dismissively. "Martial law's been declared."

The bus rolled on; the girls and the men who greeted them quieted down. I dozed. The bus stopped again, snapping me out of it. This time the high beams revealed Army Jeeps and an Army truck sitting slantways in the highway. Helmeted, armed soldiers hustled forward to bang on the passenger door. The driver opened up, then stood at the top of the stairs. I heard one of the soldiers say something about martial law, the term my grandmother had used, but loud and bossy. He said his men were going to search the bus. The driver didn't budge.

"This," he announced, "is the night bus to Dallas."

The soldier made to push past him. The driver wouldn't push. I had a back-of-my-head feeling those two negligee-clad women were trying to sink through the floorboards.

"Step aside," the soldier said.

"No, sir. Not if you're not buying a ticket. This is the night bus to Dallas and I have a schedule to keep. If you're not traveling with us, step off."

"You can't just refuse..."

"You're interfering with interstate commerce," the driver said. "I have a schedule to keep."

More was said, but they were talking quietly now. In less time than it takes to tell the soldiers got off the bus, the door hissed shut and we rolled past the roadblock. My grandmother started clapping her hands slowly. Soon the whole bus joined her applause. The driver ignored it. By the time we got to Dallas, oddments of clothing had appeared from various donors so the girls didn't cause a sensation when they got off the bus.

Of all the many things I saw on that eternally long trip, the girls stayed with me. Mainly because from time to time my grandmother would pronounce "This is the night bus to Dallas," which meant it was time to get moving, no fooling.

It was long decades and thousands of miles from the South before I wondered if my memory was accurate about that late-summer night in 1954. And by god I found the archived news stories: there *was* a Phoenix City, running wide-open flesh pots that year across the state border from military installations at Columbus, Georgia. The very month we were on the Dallas bus the governor had declared martial law because a reform-minded attorney general elect was gunned down in that Babylon of Alabama. We had brushed by history that night.

Archives say the National Guard razed whore houses, gambling parlors and other dens of iniquity. The Columbus reporter who covered the story got a Pulitzer Prize. Though there were hundreds of arrests and indictments, the main crooks moved somewhere else and went right on with their nefarious enterprises. The son of the murdered attorney general was later elected governor. It was business (elsewhere) as usual for the hoodlums; fame and fortune for the crime-busters. But the histories are silent on the fate of all the hapless whores when the National Guard rolled in followed by special prosecutors.

I can shed belated light on two: "Night bus to Dallas."

Georgia Public School

UP UNTIL THE YEAR Eisenhower ran against Adlai Stevenson for President, I led a fairly normal life for a young white boy growing up in a Georgia working-class family. That is to say that in public grade school I already had exchanged bloody noses with childhood antagonists over such weighty issues as who was the best cowboy, Gene Autry or Roy Rogers. The brick public school I attended resembled a prison. But the teachers liked me and that was a problem. The other inmates decided I was a teacher's pet and set out to punish me.

In retrospect the routine violence of those childhood days seems medieval. The only fiction I have read that accurately described the violence was the one about killing Mockingbirds. One other author touched on it. Ray Bradbury wrote a chilling tale of a father who struck a Mephistophelian bargain to be swapped for his grade-school son and endure childhood in his stead--and the horror he felt when the deal was struck and his grownup son walked away as schoolyard bullies closed in. Science fiction? Hell, no. Nightmare fiction.

The day came when I was chased home from school by a rock-throwing gang of bullying classmates led by a boy I had thought my best friend. He wasn't. He just happened to live next door. They chased me but kept their distance because I threw the rocks back. My pre-school brother was waiting at the fence for me. He instantly opened the gate to release my dog Pal. I have an indelible memory of Pal's blinding speed as he raced to me down Merry Street. The bullies ran. Pal looked like a starved coyote when I selected him from the city pound but matured into an approximate collie. Pal just was glad to see me. He didn't even notice the bullies. Later I was in awe how fast my little brother's brain operated to run such a bluff.

I cried about being bullied to my grandmother. She told my city fireman grandfather when he got home from his shift. Given his legendary fighting prowess I thought he would be contemptuous. Instead he opened his big trunk where he kept best-loved things and showed me a broken cap pistol wrapped carefully in a handkerchief. His oldest son, my uncle, was an Army captain who served with Ike against Hitler. In grade school he also was labeled teacher's pet and punished by bullies. Three were particularly vicious. My grandfather asked why he didn't fight. My uncle confessed he was afraid of the leader of the pack, let alone three on one. My grandfather sent him to school with his Depression-era pot metal cap gun and the following advice: next time they corner you, hold the cap gun in your fist and hit the leader in the face. Knock him down. Then jump the second one. The third will run; bullies are born cowards. The treasured cap gun was proof my grandfather's Georgia solution worked. My uncle was never bullied again. My grandfather approved of my return volleys of rocks and my brother's use of Pal. He thought they'd leave me alone now. They did. But they took their revenge on my dog.

Pal liked to vault up on the cement-block backyard fence to press his nose through the wire and watch for ice-cream vendors who trudged through the awful heat pushing three-wheeled magic carts of frozen goodness. When they realized he was not barking because they were black but because he was fearful his humans would miss the cart and not get his daily ice cream, they saved out broken bars to feed him.

Bullies are nothing if not obsessively observant about their prey. They hid beneath the fence where the vendors fed Pal, and called him. His brain said ice cream. He bolted toward them. I saw a spark and curl of smoke and screamed for him to stop. But he was already pressing his nose in the wire.

The string of firecrackers exploded right in his face.

He yelped, fell off the fence and ran under the house. He wouldn't come out. The last dog that ran under the house and wouldn't come out was so badly injured my grandfather took him somewhere and shot him. I was so angry I could hardly think. I headed for my neighbor's house and screamed for him to come out. My brother, now approaching his seventieth year, says "I only remember that you called him out. Not why." That was why.

My enemy stood on a curbing around his lawn log mouthing off until I lowered my fists. Then he leaped on me. We went down, him on top. He fastened his teeth in the pad of my thumb and chomped down. The pain was shocking. I flailed punches with my other fist. I cried. From pain, but mostly because I couldn't hurt him the way he clung to me like a leech.

My mother had followed me. Now she grabbed his ankles and dragged him loose. He took a chunk of flesh with him. "Damn you fight fair!" she yelled. By the time I got to my feet he was up on his porch, saying I don't fight boys who *cry.* Can a third-grader feel homicidal rage? I went after him. He ran inside, slammed the screen door and latched it. I was trying to yank it off its hinges when my mother and grandmother pulled me off. They said I could not invade his house. That I had won, let's go home. They had to drag me.

Poor Pal was not severely burned. But ever after, any sudden noise sent him hiding in the bathtub, terrified. Bullying toward me, however, stopped. Before I could enjoy it, I came out of school to find two boys holding a friend of mine spread- eagled over the outdoor drinking fountain while a fifth-grader beat him with a leather belt. I said you can't do that to *my* friend. So he slashed me across the face with the buckle. Man, it hurt!

And the fight was on. Sort of a fight. He kept slashing me. I couldn't get close enough to hit him. There was a pile of bricks for school repairs. I grabbed two and threw with more fury than accuracy. He ducked. I threw two more. He decided to retreat from the pile. So I held one in each hand and chased him while he bobbed and weaved and tried to laugh. I kept coming and he stopped laughing. When I grazed his arm with a brick he ran away. His confederates were long gone. So was my friend.

My facial lacerations persuaded my family Georgia public schools were not for me. Since they weren't quite ready to move to Florida where they believed schools more civilized, somehow they found the money to send me to parochial school.

Their hearts were in the right place. But I discovered that trouble followed me like that black cloud above the Al Capp cartoon character's head. The parochial-school principal was a wise woman and practicing psychologist.

She patted me on the shoulder and said being paranoid didn't mean I didn't have real enemies. I wasn't sure what the fancy word meant, but I always remembered her words.

Seawall Code

SHE WAS A LEGGY older woman with long raven-dark tresses who lived across Palm Place and wore tight black pants and men's white dress shirts with the top buttons unbuttoned over the swell of large firm breasts. She was the first woman I knew who never wore a bra. She was very proud of her ability to whistle shrilly through her teeth louder than any man. The odd things you remember. Her husband was quite ill and seldom seen outside. She was fairly plain as far as looks but to a horny teenage virgin she exuded sex like an aroma. I was terrified of her.

I was working days as a copy boy at the city newspaper and nights at home on my first novel. Of course my family had to tell everybody I was a writer. This embarrassed the hell out of me because the first question from anybody would be: what do you write? Mention science-fiction and adults would go "Oh" and lose interest. Even the sophisticated mother of my hunting buddy, who trained for the diplomat corps before she married and spoke fluent French, asked me point-blank: does it have any sex in it? I remember blushing and saying no.

"Then it'll never sell," Cricket's mom pronounced.

So I was careful who I spoke to about my writing. I didn't want to talk about writing, I wanted to write. We lived two doors from the beach. The ocean was my muse. When I got stuck I walked up to the seawall to think and watch waves. After she learned I was writing, every time I walked to the beach the leggy lady from across Palm Place would show up to talk about writing. She evidently read quite a lot but said she didn't understand science-fiction. I wasn't about to try to explain it. She wanted to know if I ever tried "real" fiction. I gave my stock reply: I didn't know enough about real life, but my imagination was equal to anybody's. She found that amusing, and said maybe I should get out experiencing some real life so I could write about it. Now, as she said this, she was sitting on the seawall bench leaning forward, elbows on knees covered by the long shirt-tails of her men's shirt, with the three top buttons undone. It was hard not to stare at her abundant breasts. Was it a come-on? How the hell do I know?

The cool sea breeze--I was sure that was what caused it--created two symmetrical tents in the oxford cloth of her shirt the size of my thumb. I felt my face burn. I was sure that if she noticed the instant bulge in my pants she would be so offended she might call a cop. Or worse, my grandmother. I turned my back and said I needed to go for a walk on the beach. I politely declined her offer to go with me, explaining I needed to be thinking, not carrying on a conversation. She just smiled and nodded and didn't even act offended at my abrupt departure. I walked far enough for the swelling to subside and then a little farther. I didn't turn back until I saw her vacate the seawall.

The next time I was on the seawall staring out to sea I heard someone come down the path from Palm Place. Then I didn't hear them. Nobody came past me to the steps down to the beach. When I turned to look, there she was, sitting with her black-clad knees demurely together under the shirt-tails and her chin in one palm, watching me silently. I said hi. She said I didn't want to interrupt your thinking, I like watching you think. She scared the hell out of me.

Another resident of Palm Place was a hard-drinking construction contractor who traveled the Southeast and told everybody I reminded him of Robert Ruark, a North Carolina writer who was in his heyday. I knew Ruark's writing from *Field and Stream* and liked it, and was secretly flattered. But the leggy lady disagreed. She said he had the right state, wrong writer. She said my stormy expressions and long-legged walks on the beach reminded her of Thomas Wolfe. Had I ever read Thomas Wolfe? I had not. You should, she said. I think you will see yourself in him.

The days drifted by and it became her common seawall question: had I yet read *Look Homeward, Angel* or any of Wolfe's other books she recommended. I had not. I was closing in on my last chapter with no interest in extraneous reading just then. She said he writes about his experiences as a young man and you could too. I reminded her I didn't have any experiences to write about. You will, she said; Wolfe's young man meets this one female character and you could learn a lot from her.

And there she let it lay, though she didn't stop recommending Thomas Wolfe. Sometimes it seemed she was speaking in some kind of code. Her presence on the seawall across the summer was disturbing, but not in a bad way. I covertly enjoyed her attention and missed her when she didn't show up. There was a humming tension between us on the seawall that I had no idea how to interpret, but it felt nice.

When I finished my book I spent a lot of time editing and retyping a clean draft, a grind that kept me off the seawall with my nose in the typewriter days on end. Our chance encounters there became less frequent and then stopped. The first editor I sent the manuscript bought it immediately. In the ensuing excitement I forgot all about Thomas Wolfe. I didn't read him until much later, after the leggy sexy lady with the sick husband had moved on. I discovered Wolfe's principal female character, Esther Jacks, was an older experienced woman who initiated the young writer into the erotic mysteries of womanhood. I experienced a jolt of recognition followed instantly by regret. I finally had cracked the seawall code, forever too late.

The Milkman's Son

A DECADE AND A HALF into the 21st Century, the local small-newspaper in my small town is a doughty anachronism that can barely muster a full page of classified ads. Most display advertising takes the form of annoying inserts that scatter all over the floor when you open the paper. Local news content is hard to distinguish from "Hundred Years Ago Today" nostalgia. For instance today's big front-page story features high school graduates with the best Grade Point Average with an attractive photo of each and thumbnail sketch of achievements, dreams and college scholarships. One of them is going to Harvard.

Harvard flashed me back half a century to my own high school on the other side of the country and my only classmate awarded a Harvard scholarship. The milkman's son; I hadn't thought of him in years. We identified classmates back then by their father's occupation: the lawyer's son, the dentist's son, the cash-register salesman's son; the milkman's son.

Back then the milkman in his little truck still delivered fresh bottles of milk daily to your front door. As his son grew into his lanky stooped height, you saw him early summer mornings, braced in his father's milk truck door at dawn. He was giving his dad a break by running bottles of milk to the doorstep and retrieving empties. He was one of the first of us to score a real summer job; working at Penny Burger.

Where his vast, questing intelligence came from was

unanswerable to me as a new and assiduous student of Mendel's theories. I could perceive no genetic connection to his unimaginative father and mother, other than work ethic. When he wasn't working, he was reading. His tastes were eclectic. He was my only classmate who quoted Kerouac. Aldous Huxley was one of his favorites. His personal role model was the Savage in *Brave New World*.

Stupidity agonized the intellectual milkman's son; he struggled with arbitrary society norms as imposed by teachers. We were the war-babies, last generation before baby-boomers exploded upon history. Eisenhower-era conformity was our great bugaboo, beatniks our unadmitted heroes. We wanted to be non-conformist but most of us were afraid to, already resigned to Henry David Thoreau's life of quiet desperation. I for one did not understand how teachers could introduce us to free-thinkers like Thoreau while ignoring the implications; but all I did was wonder. The milkman's son took action to challenge the status-quo.

He came to school senior year wearing a Mohawk haircut.

The sensation that caused had to be lived through to be believed. Word had spread to alert us to his stunt; there were eyes in every homeroom window to watch his characteristic lunging, head-thrust-forward stride up the front walk.

The vice-principal stood in the door to bar entry.

Unlike Arkansas where Eisenhower enforced desegregation, the milkman's son did not have the 82nd Airborne backing him. No massive television-news cameras showed up. Intellectual non-conformity did not have the federal-court vogue that race did.

The morning bell rang. The gorilla-like vice-principal led the milkman's son inside with a meaty hand on frail, stooped shoulder. He kept paddles big as cricket bats in his office with random holes drilled in the wood to cause flesh to pucker painfully when he landed a blow. But this was a different kind of morning. The entire school buzzed from top to bottom like disturbed bees; the hum was distinctly audible. Teachers refused to answer questions about the fate of the milkman's son and tried to impose order.

About lunchtime things settled down. The grapevine whispered that he somehow avoided the brutal paddles but had been expelled for his unthinkable breach of conformity. Some students were angry that an honors student could be expelled like a common trouble-maker; good grades were supposed to protect you. But a surprising number railed loudly against his rebellion, making sure the powers-that-be heard and saw what good little subjects they were.

His parents were called in. Adults struck a compromise behind closed doors. If his parents would force him to shave off the Mohawk, he could return to class. They did, and he did; he was *completely bald* when he came back, wearing his trademark sardonic grin at plebeian stupidity. In Florida, where everyone had some degree of tan, his bald dome glowed bluish-white and alien; startlingly large. To science-fiction fans he resembled a denizen of some tomorrow where brains were more important than brawn. School went on; the sensation gradually faded. By Christmas break his hair grew back as a sparse smudge, not much shorter than conformist crew-cuts.

When he came back to school in January he had shaved

his head entirely bald again. His mobile lips curled in titanic inner amusement at the enraged reaction of school functionaries. They decreed bald was acceptable, he pointed out – so he was just following orders. Their frustrated fury was monumental. The milkman's son had neatly tied their hands and thereby created a legend for himself. They would be watching him like a hawk from now on.

His small circle of friends secretly admired not only his courage but his wit. We were all great fans of Eric Frank Russell, a science-fiction writer whose maverick characters always screwed with hidebound authority and would have recognized the milkman's son as one of them. I was the only one who grasped the sensitive soul beneath the legend and wondered if he would weaken under constant pressure from vengeful authority, and emulate the Savage in *Brave New World*. That is to say be found hanged, a suicide, his toes slowly tracing the points of the compass...

Instead he went to Harvard on a scholarship.

When the award was announced, authorities proved consistency is the hobgoblin of small minds as Mencken wrote; they muttered about the scandalous development and predicted he would come to no good end.

In this new century, when body-pierced and tattooed non-conformity is the new conformity, the revolt of the milkman's son seems bland. But it was earth-shattering in the last year of the Eisenhower presidency. Guess you had to be there.

Blondie

BLONDIE WAS NOT PART of my Florida of swamps and hammocks and Flatwoods forests, and gators that stole ducks we shot and frightful water moccasins as thick as my arm. She was a beach dweller and sun lover. She raised Daschunds instead of children and owned many nice things. She named her dogs for a Broadway show, and you could hear Colonel Pickering and Eliza barking as the three of them came up the lane. The Colonel was the only Daschund I ever heard of that ran off a Doberman that invaded his back yard. He was some sausage dog, the Colonel.

Blondie was in her fifties but her breasts were firm and tip-tilty as a co-ed's. I knew this because she stood naked in front of her boudoir mirror next door and daily combed her hair the obligatory strokes to keep it beautiful. I had a perfect line of sight from our upstairs bathroom through the branches of a giant palm tree; my personal peep show.

My grandmother said drily that Blondie spent more money on her body than she spent raising four kids and two grandkids. For some reason, Blondie and my grandmother got along very well; they seemed to have an unspoken understanding which confused my teenage sensibility. Blondie was Florida sex appeal walking; my grandmother was dried out by the sun and bent from a lifetime of toil. I was too young to realize perhaps Blondie reminded her of her lost flapper youth, when she had been the girlfriend of a Rumrunner chieftain. Hell, I didn't even know the half of her complicated history then.

Though Blondie was almost as old as my grandmother, when you saw her walking saucily away from you with that cloud of bright gold hair whipping in the sea wind, you'd swear it was a slim young woman. The Beaches legend was that she started as an upstairs maid for one of the rich Jacksonville families that kept a beach house, and worked her way up. She spent time as a traveling companion for wealthy men who took trips to Miami and Havana and preferred a blonde, beautiful traveling companion. She still worked very hard at staying blonde and beautiful. She knew secrets about anybody on the Beaches it was worth knowing secrets about, so nobody troubled her about the young women she groomed to go on the road as she had. In good weather, her backyard hosted one continuous running party, like the Alabama Tiger's boat in Travis McGee novels, where curvaceous young women came and went with hard-drinking executives and naval officers.

Her fitness regimen was vigorous yard work under the brutal Florida sun in shorts and a sleeveless top. She did all the yard work for a rich lawyer's oceanfront spread. Waggish neighbors said she did the bed work too, because Mrs. Lawyer was sick all the time. My personal hero was the lawyer's rakehell son who seemed to have a bevy of beauties on call. I was too naïve to wonder if Blondie doubled down with the son. For all the sexual energy that blossomed like oleander under the Florida sun I was unwillingly ignorant of the ways of the flesh.

One day Blondie told me out of the blue she would like to go for a ride on my motor scooter. Holy smokes. I had never had a girl on the jump seat. Then it's about time she said. I kicked the old Cushman to life despite a tremor in my leg. She was wearing jeans that day to avoid getting burned by the hot exhaust; she had come prepared. I wished furiously my scooter could magically become a blazing fast BMW cycle like one of my friends had.

But no; it putt-putted away at walking speed, then running speed, and finally up to around thirty mph, its absolute top end. Her long lean legs were snugged around my hips and she leaned into me with those work-toned arms wrapped around my middle. When we passed plate glass windows and I saw that glorious blonde hair streaming behind while she hugged me, I almost had a religious experience. She rode well, leaning with me on turns, and I wished I could ride forever or at least until everybody on the Beaches saw us. When we got back she was smiling quietly and seemed happy. I didn't know what to do with myself.

"You took me for a ride on your motor scooter," she said. "It's only fair I take you for a ride in my MG."

Holy smokes twice. Was there anything cooler than those little MG convertibles? If there was I couldn't think of it. I clumped behind her trim figure like a plowboy jumping furrows; like a circus bear following a ballerina.

She flipped me the keys. "You drive," she said.

Oh god. My life flashed before my eyes. How humiliating to admit I had never driven a stick shift. I waited for ridicule.

"You drive and I'll shift," she said.

Back in those dark sexually repressed days before the sixties, I had read movie reviews about celluloid symbolism for sex: Robert Mitchum releasing a stallion into the paddock with a mare while his hooded gaze held the heroine motionless--fade to black. A woman kneeling in front of a seated man playing a saxophone between his legs. That kind of thing.

I worked the clutch while her left hand engulfed the short gear lever that was so close her knuckles rubbed against my right thigh, shifting briskly. She would say, "Punch it. Now!" We got into a rhythm and that little MG flew. Having a good-looking woman's hand rubbing my leg so close to my groin, the spasmodic leaps of the car as I learned the clutch and her exclamations felt so much like one of those symbolic Hollywood moments I had a painful erection by the time we got back. I had to sit for a while before I could climb out without embarrassing myself. Blondie just smiled and said we'll have to do that again sometime. We never did but I knew I would never forget that ride.

The following New Year's, Blondie kissed me.

Such a simple statement freighted with so much meaning.

The adults around Palm Place wandered from house to house on New Year's Eve, drinking and making merry. My grandmother strictly enforced an old Georgia superstition that a dark-haired man must be the first to enter the home when the New Year struck. Blondie's date was a dark-haired man so she dragged him over to fulfill the ritual. I was at my typewriter in the corner as usual, trying to ignore the distractions.

Blondie leaned over, took my face between her hands, and kissed me right on the lips. She was the first woman who ever kissed me. She did it thoroughly, with mobile lips and tongue. If I had been standing, my knees would have buckled. Then it was as if a relay had closed somewhere in my brain and I kissed her back. Time stood still. My lips asked and hers answered. In a way I have never been able to explain, that kiss was pure magic. It was first kiss, all kisses, a thousand remembered kisses, as if her lips and tongue stripped Lethe's veil from memory and awakened me to past lives full of marvelous kisses. Then it was over and she straightened up and patted me on the head and said "Happy New Year."

I didn't do any more writing that night. But the second time a woman kissed me, this time with carnal intent, on a frozen Christmas Eve in Paris my lips knew exactly what to do.

Jacksonville
Rail Terminal 1967

DEADENING HEAT OF LATE JULY slashed by the orgasmic release of a Florida thunderstorm, with rain sheeting in feathery wind-frothed fury. Six frantic lunging steps from the taxi to the shelter of the Jacksonville Rail Terminal is six too many to escape being drenched. Inside the annex the steel roof shudders under peals of thunder.

The terminal is crowded for a summer afternoon. Big silver Coast Line trains ease into the storm with lordly disdain for hurrying clocks. It has been a long time since American trains ran on time. Expressways and jet airliners sapped their utility and defeated their pride. The flooring is old and worn. A television perches anachronistically above the waiting room for all to watch. A honey-voiced male announcer, throwback to an earlier era, makes it known a train scheduled to depart at 5:05 is ready for passengers; the station clock says 4:35. Rain falters and stops but thick clouds hang unresolved and thunder fidgets. Even inside the terminal the heat seeps back around the sticky edges of dripping humidity.

Big white-painted bumpers guard the terminus of tracks against the station platform. Each mounts a miniature palm tree in a concrete pot like table decorations at a banquet long over. Tired dun mail cars contrast with silver passenger coaches against the bumpers. A jumping

135

neon arrow points arrivals toward *Hertz; Cocktails; Redcap Service; Dining Room.*

Out by the tracks the PA system is garbled by static. Passengers take their places like extras on a movie set. The historic Silver Meteor is called for "Savannah ... Petersburg ... Washington ... Baltimore." Pause. "Annnd ... *New* York City."

Miniature palm trees, the Silver Meteor and static-filled calls offer a fleeting glimpse of Old Florida. Slumping passengers give off a feeling they are waiting for a train they missed twenty years ago. They look resigned to the fact they're not going to catch it today.

American railroad men have grown old; conductors, redcaps, everybody. Redcaps act hateful to passengers as if they resent outliving the salad days of American rail. No more mobsters take the Silver Meteor to Miami for the winter, spreading largesse like hoodlum royalty. No more desert sheiks wearing wealth on their fingers, to feed the legend of waitresses tipped with large emeralds. No more stingy captains of American industry to assert a good tip is "Be kind to your mother."

Hard to pinpoint when it all began to go sour. When Flappers stopped dancing the Charleston? When the feds finally jailed Capone? When Repeal came in and drinking stopped being an act of civil disobedience that was fun? When the market crashed and the long dreary Depression began? When the giddy excitement of the Second World War ended and heroes hung up their dashing uniforms, married and settled in subdivision houses? When their former commanding general decided to emulate the dictator they whipped and build autobahns all over America and Detroit filled the concrete with huge chrome-burnished automobiles?

Probably all of the above, drip by drip like Chinese water torture. "Life was more fun back then," grouses an ageing sybarite. "Now it's all dull. Just dull. The whole world is dull."

Little by little the terminal crowd thins until the whine of electric-eye doors is clearly audible when someone enters or leaves. The PA announces a westbound train: "DeFuniak Springs ... Mobile ... Biloxi ..." Dramatic pause. "And Newww Orleans!"

A phone rings unanswered in closed Coast Line offices. It rings and rings.

Miscellaneous Cop Stories

Small-Town
Police Chief

IT WAS THE TALES OF THE OLD SALTS that did it. Navy men with a sea swagger in their walk as they ambled through the small town in Pennsylvania, their speech crowded with an exotic imagery of far-flung and magical places beyond the sheltering hills.

The sailors came to landlocked Bucknell University at the south end of town to teach college boys who signed up for the reserves rope-splicing and knot-tying and basic seamanship and drill and ceremonies. When they hit the grub line in the dining hall on campus—which they persisted in calling the galley—young Don H., who worked on the food line when he wasn't carrying water buckets for the Bucknell Eleven at football games, eavesdropped on their yarning.

Quick as he was old enough, he joined the Navy to see that wide world. He left his grandparents' boarding house (rooms to let for college students) and his BB gun behind. (The one city cop they had back then confiscated his BB gun over a misunderstanding about a streetlight or two when he was thirteen, but gave it back when he promised to behave ...)

Well, he saw the world. After he changed services, swapping bellbottom sailor pants for Marine fatigues, he saw more of it than he would have liked, in and around a nasty cold peninsula named Korea that was swarming with more hostile Red Chinese than it was easy to comprehend.

He survived that, and more years in service, winding up in the Counterintelligence Corps before he put on a civilian police uniform in nearby counties. All through those years, sun-dappled summers in sleepy Lewisberg, and its quiet snow-covered winters, loomed larger and lovelier in his mind's eye. He had seen the wide world. Lewisberg looked a lot better now.

Gazing out over a main drag that hadn't changed a lot from old black-and-white photos on the wall of the police station, he remembered his yearning at age 43 to return to the scene of his fully-lived childhood in a place that needed only a single policemen that everyone knew by first name. When he secured the appointment to chief, he thought he had it made.

But appearances deceived. He now commanded an eight-man police force with radio cars and walkie talkies and a full arsenal of firepower. Lewisberg had grown to 6,200, by the last census, and the surrounding townships had grown too.

But mainly, now, there was "this Berrigan business."

A federal penitentiary stood on the northern outskirts of town, largely unremarked until a Roman Catholic priest named Philip Berrigan was imprisoned there, for anti-war activities concerning another nasty little Asian war that grew like Topsy. From his cell, the government now alleged, the priest had masterminded a violent kidnap-bombing plot against the nation's capital to protest the Vietnam Conflict.

Other priests and nuns—and Bucknell students and one doctor of philosophy, and others, academic and not, named and unnamed—slipped into this out-of-the way small town to plot, and to receive instructions smuggled from the ringleader's cell. So ran the indicting narrative. A Bucknell prisoner on study-release—a con man by his record—was the conspirators' courier. But he was working a double-game as an agent provocateur, according to Jack Nelson of the Los Angeles Times, and would be the star witness when a federal trial convened in Harrisburg.

"The press calls them the Harrisburg Six, don't they?" The small-town police chief shook his head, perhaps at his vanished dream of a peaceful return to earlier times. "Not the Lewisburg Six? Good. I hope this all stays down there in Harrisburg. We don't need that trial, or anything to do with it, here. This one we got right now is enough!"

"This one" was a trial of Black Muslim convicts from the federal pen, accused of clubbing and stomping guards in a savage prison uprising. His small police force was charged with security in and around the second-floor courthouse, just down the main drag from borough council offices.

It was a larger courtroom than the federal ones in Harrisburg, he noted. Several side doors provided access from an open hallway—the hallway reachable by an open stairwell and an elevator. No electronic surveillance tools like in Harrisburg, no barricades—just a thorough frisk by his muscular plainclothesmen, big hands rough and clinical and no respecter of personal privacy. Physical security the old-fashioned way: gimlet-eyed cops at the head of the stairwell and the elevator door, with no physical barriers to hide behind.

"We had a real scare one day," the chief mused. "One of the guys on courtroom duty saw a guy across the street in an apartment building with a rifle. We went out there and surrounded it and went in with shotguns. It turned out to be the renter, cleaning his deer rifle. He'd just moved over to the window to catch the light down the barrel. But we were shook."

He stared off across the afternoon. "There was a time, not all that long ago, when you could just about sit on the steps of the courthouse and clean your deer rifle if you wanted to and nobody would even look up. But it's different now."

Very different. His small force had already been required to escort a protest march of anti-war demonstrators down the street to the federal courthouse, and stand around listening to harangues and a few anti-war songs—while the tense Black Muslim trial continued inside—then watch seven young men in the group march up to the Selective Service Office to turn in their draft cards.

He shook his head again. "I guess you could say that all my life I was migrating home to Lewisburg the way I remembered it."

His grandparents churned homemade ice cream in the hot summers, and the boarding-room students liked that a lot. There was a bakery next door run by the family of the now-borough secretary. Her husband was a Bucknell student who came to study and stayed to marry and make a small-town life. She and the chief remembered that Bucknell had about 1,200 students back then—less than half the enrollment now—and none of them had been out in the streets raising hell about any wars then.

"We didn't even know the federal prison was letting prisoners out into the community like this guy who carried letters for that priest," the woman said now. "There's a lot of bad feeling in the town about that. We should have been told."

"The first thing I knew about that—or about this whole Berrigan business," the chief said, "was when I started getting calls from all those big newspapers. The town's been on edge ever since."

He showed one of his visitors a faded police citation form dated 1941 that concerned street lights and BB guns. Two Daisies had been confiscated from one Donald H.

"That was our big crime wave back then," he said drily.

The console on his clerk's desk emitted static, then terse communications from two units on patrol near the courthouse. Another crowd seemed to be gathering. He reached for his hat.

"I'll be glad when this nonsense is over," he said. "Then maybe it will feel like I'm finally home for good."

Mistaken Identity

THE TWENTY-FIRST CENTURY plunges headlong into a future that increasingly resembles the worst nightmares of science fiction writers deep in the twentieth. Ray Bradbury for instance was usually irrepressible but foresaw sinister armored cops empowered to stop and interrogate any pedestrian out for a stroll and "disappear" them if they didn't measure up. His more-famous *Fahrenheit 451* was about firemen charged with burning books to enforce illiteracy. Naming book-burners firemen was a fine example of Orwellian newspeak. But postulating a government trying to force illiteracy on its subjects seems as quaint as Lewis Carroll's Red Queen.

With the advent of TV, computers, cell phones and all the tweeting spawn of electronic "social media," the great unwashed do not need official protection from literacy. They race to embrace it with the sure suicidal urge of lemmings for the sea. George Orwell's *1984* was the poster child for government thought-control. When the year itself came and went pundits guilty of sloppy thinking pronounced the threat over, like that of the Mayan doomsday prophecies. But inhabitants of this not-so-brave New World *voluntarily* carry electronic devices that pinpoint their moment-to-moment location with enough precision to be eliminated by a drone strike if they annoy some faceless bureaucrat.

Thoughtful safeguards designed to protect a free

citizenry by power-wary Rebels who threw off a mad English King's yoke are routinely ignored or circumvented by today's powers-that-be, enthroned in their electronic-warfare palaces. Entrepreneurial electronics salesmen constantly rush new devices into the hands of the new police state for purchase by taxpayer dollars to help control the wage-slaves. The allegedly free press is less concerned with watchdogging government and more worried about their revenue streams and loss of classified advertising to Craig's List as the public embraces the toys of the electronic age.

Any group that tries to stand against the rising tide of vanishing liberty is quickly demonized and marginalized by spin doctors with skills and equipment to make Orwell's Big Brother weep for envy. The term "tea party," borrowed from the colonial rebellion against taxes viewed as onerous, has been Goebbels-massaged to mean dangerous crank if not domestic terrorist. Never mind the savage adherents of a sixth-century caravan raider's twisted religion...focus on flyover country, occupied by crew-cut Bible-thumping gun-clutching bogeymen, probably racist and homophobic, and assuredly not nice people! Be sure to ask the computer about them.

The cops were among the first to embrace the electronic age. Before there were body cams and a cellphone camera in every hand, they linked their two-way radios to computers to dispense street justice. One incident that never made primetime because the victim was white and middle-class and sans constituency sticks in my mind as a forerunner of today. The citizen in question was disturbed by thunderously loud music being played next door. He called the cops for help.

The first thing the cops did was run *him* through their data-banks to see if he was worth paying attention to. As it developed, some bored keyboardist in the faceless bowels of bureaucracy had failed to keep computer entries on this citizen up to date. The computer told responding officers the complainant had an outstanding warrant against him for an old relatively minor beef. So when the complainant greeted the cops expecting help with the loud music, they told him he was under arrest. When they told him what for, he got upset and said that beef was settled long ago and the warrant dismissed. Cops already believed their computers like the ancients believed Delphi. They tried to apply the cuffs. He resisted, protesting they were making a mistake. So they choked him out. They were a little too enthusiastic. They killed him. It was one way to keep him from having to listen to the objectionably loud music.

The after-action report vindicated the victim's veracity. Oops. One might think the cops would begin to worry about their computers' accuracy. Nope. The lesson the public was instructed to take from this was no matter how mistaken the cops, you must fall to your knees or your belly and obey. Being right is no defense. Scandal, law suits as a result of such abuse? *Hell,* no. The cops were cleared because their absolute defense was *they believed the computer over the human.* In this century this is the norm. It has been a long time since anyone uttered the punch-card phrase of the nineteen fifties—"garbage in, garbage out." Today it is humanity—and any fading memory of a free citizenry—that is folded, spindled and mutilated.

Nobody anymore reads those old cautionary science-fiction tales about computer- enhanced authority run amuck, vanished now with other ephemera of the fifties: Brylcreme (a little dab will do ya!), NeHi grape soda and tailfins on cars. Not to mention a war-hero President who warned that the military-industrial complex was a far worse threat to liberty than the Nazis his armies defeated. The devices built by the electronic industry for the government make him a prophet. Speaking of which, Nazis would still be polishing up their Three Thousand Year Reich if the Gestapo had the electronic suite of suppression tools available to American cops today. Devices already deployed and new ones coming on line daily without any objective monitoring, read like a Hitler wet dream.

This whole diatribe came pouring off my keyboard triggered by an unlikely source: in rambling through my writer's notes of a lifetime I stumbled across a twenty-five-year old field-contact report from an agency for which I once played spin doctor, tucked away thinking it might provide grist for a story someday. Computers and electronics were involved peripherally in the incident. The reason for the report's length and self-justification however was simple bad luck.

A salty female Patrol sergeant's bad behavior had exploded into headlines. (Newspapers were still a going concern at the time.) Except for certain factual mistakes she made, she had done nothing unusual in the situation. But she had the bad luck to do it to major campaign contributors for the sitting governor. Ka-boom. It was evident she could feel her promising career slipping away in the aftermath and applied her report-writing skills to try to forestall it.

On this rainy March evening at 6:39 p.m., she wrote: "Communications advised County Deputy R.K. G—. was northbound I-5 … requesting backup. He was following a gray Honda Accord, License 342-BKD, that had been reported brandishing a shotgun at other vehicles, starting at mile post 95 northbound ….”

Has anyone ever seen a Honda Accord brandish a shotgun? Cop-speak; it's a language of its own. I once enrolled in a university police-reporting class to try to trace its roots. My Military Police School instructors in 1965 recommended simple declarative sentences in plain English. I discussed this with my college instructor, a county lieutenant himself. He said no one knew the genesis of this stilted writing. He concurred with the MP instructors at Fort Gordon. But he said once cops were turned loose on the road these strange writing habits appeared out of thin air.

“Trooper C. T. F—. was standing by at 84th Street,” the sergeant's report went on. Another report-writing error: she assumed all readers would know she meant the 84th Street on-ramp to I-5. A mere quibble you say? Have *you* ever been cross-examined by a defense attorney? But let it ride. “Trooper Gene C--. and I stood by at SR 512. As Deputy G--. passed, he advised he was directly behind the vehicle.”

Here, another aside. The late 1980s had seen media hysteria develop about “road rage,” shorthand for random highway shootings. As a Patrol bureaucrat at the time charged with dealing with the media, I knew there was heated internal debate about whether to report such incidents or pretend they didn't happen, to cool down the rhetoric. To the Patrol's credit, the decision was in favor of accurate reporting and let the chips fall. Who knows how cops do these things now?

"At this time it was dark and raining heavily, visibility was poor," the report goes on. "I observed the dark compact directly ahead in front of Deputy G--.'s vehicle, in Lane 3. I directed C--., F--. And G--. To block off lanes 2, 3 and 4 behind the vehicle, as traffic was fairly heavy.

"I directed the felony stop to take place north of 72nd, as it was a wide shoulder and had a straight visual approach for on-coming traffic. We would block Lane 1 and the shoulder, parking 40 to 50 feet behind the vehicle. Four people were visible. As we coordinated the stop, Communications advised numerous reports of the vehicle brandishing a shotgun—and there was no record of the license I had called out, 342 BKO..." Reasonably straightforward, though the reader had to infer the four people referred to were in the target car. But notice the license-plate number she used.

"We stopped the vehicle at 6:44 p.m. at the above location. All police personnel took cover between engine blocks and open driver's doors, with handguns drawn, I advised the occupants in the vehicle to raise their hands so they were visible. I then directed the driver to take the ignition keys out with his left hand and drop them out the window, he complied..." Succinct, to the point, poor punctuation notwithstanding.

"I then had the driver exist the vehicle and directed him to face forward, he complied with the request. I had him back up to my Patrol car on the shoulder with his hands in the air. It was still raining heavily, so I did not make him assume the prone position, but had Trooper F--. Cuff him, standing." Here's where she began defense of her actions, by volunteering that she was being nice not to prone him out in the rainy dark on a busy freeway. After all, the radio told her he was a bad guy, right? The driver was searched for weapons and placed in Trooper C--.'s car next to the sergeant's.

The woman in the right-front seat was treated the same way, cuffed (standing, she made sure to point out) and put in the sergeant's car. Two heads left in the car, but then the sergeant saw mysterious "curly white hair raise up between them and disappear..."

No comment about how this curly white apparition affected her emotions, her judgment or the tone of her voice. But she reported trouble with the second male passenger. He "exited with his back toward us and hands lowered and not visible. I told him to raise his hands above his head. He turned around to face us and raised his hands. I directed him to turn around. After several more directions he did face forward. While he was backing toward the Patrol cars, he continually disregarded the directions, turning to face us twice more and lowering and hiding his hands from us..."

They didn't like this. When he reached them, one of the troopers cuffed his left hand (again standing, she carefully noted) and the guy started to turn around again. "F--. Had to face him forward...F--. Later advised me he resisted getting into the car. The Deputy assisted F--. In getting him into the car." Note the verbs. Resistance, assistance; nothing to suggest a scuffle. The second woman "followed directions well," the sergeant noted.

"I then directed the other occupant (white hair) out. Trooper F--. Advised me the occupants said it was a dog. The woman in my Patrol car confirmed this. C--. And F--.

Approached the car and discovered the only other occupant was a dog...."

Beginning to sound absurd yet? The sergeant carefully recorded that she explained to her prisoner why they had been stopped this way "and she stated she understood." Right, Sarge; she forgave you your trespasses, in handcuffs in a back-seat with no door handle, with four drawn guns in evidence.

"C--. And F--. Began to search for a shotgun, when Radio advised the vehicle had two occupants and the license (newly reported) was 342-BKD. The vehicle we stopped was 342-BKO...." This is where an attorney (or a good reporter) would begin to have a field day. "Newly reported?" Then why did the sergeant's report correctly identify the suspect plate in first reference? Which was accurate? Did they have the right number and stop the wrong car and fail to notice right away, or did Radio give them the wrong number and now was correcting? Her subsequent actions are suggestive. The sergeant went to see what her search-team was finding and observed the frantic white pooch "jumping all over inside the car." This was gratuitously reported to explain how spilled drinks got all over the interior of the car; no fault of the cops, see?

"Radio had also advised the occupants were 'drinking,'" the sergeant said. "C--. Was smelling a paper Pepsi cup's content, recapped it and replaced it on the right floorboard. No shotgun was found." The way the report is written, they already knew they had the wrong car, so Radio's reporting whoever allegedly was waving a shotgun around had been drinking was irrelevant. Ah, but if this wrongfully-stopped group had some alcohol in their cups, maybe some damage control was possible; you have read between the lines here. The report deteriorates even more.

"Radio then advised updated reports indicated the license to be 392-BKP." Meaning the actual suspect vehicle, one has to infer, since it's not made clear. "I ran the VIN. As I contacted the driver, Radio advised no record of the VIN. (Vehicle Identification Number; no explanation for running the VIN of a car now known to be the wrong one.) I then advised the driver why we had stopped them in this fashion. He seemed surprised and stated he didn't even own a handgun. I asked if we could look in his trunk and he said yes. No shotgun was located."

Getting the picture yet? Compounded stupidities. Even if there *had* been a shotgun in the trunk, it would have proved...precisely nothing. Why search the wrong vehicle?

"I then had all occupants released immediately, explained again and got their names and other information..." The Honda Accord they thought they had stopped turned out to be, in fact, a Chevy Nova. Not only the wrong plate, they stopped the wrong make of car. "Gathering the information from the occupants, I again explained the situation and continually apologized for the happenings. I explained in the rain and darkness we couldn't tell the vehicle was a Nova. The (back-seat passengers) were continually hostile and aggressive. (The male) stated he'd been a dispatcher for Santa Clara or Santa Cruz Police and our behavior was ridiculous. I asked him how many police officers had been killed during traffic stops...he acknowledged traffic stops a leader in police-officer fatalities, but our techniques were extreme..."

Nobody likes negative criticism, particularly so well-warranted. "I advised him he had been extremely uncooperative, not following directions, turning during cuffing, and that our officer-safety measures were only the minimum to ensure his compliance..."

In plain English, she argued with him. "His wife started screaming at me that she was a citizen. She was overreacting..." Overreacting. Overreacting to being stopped in the wrong kind of car, with the wrong license plate, having guns pointed at her and cuffed and confined, after what had been a pleasant drive to the beach. Fortunately no one was choked to death for overreacting.

The final full page of the report was devoted to self-justification. It asserted the front-seat people were understanding. That they disapproved the anger expressed by their friends in the back seat. The sergeant could not resist sticking in just in case that the front-seaters had in fact been drinking. One has to infer she meant alcohol. A lot of what was said at roadside didn't get into the report. I heard the other side of the story from the Seattle *Times* reporter who interviewed the two couples. Unfortunately for the sergeant, her supervisor had already signed off on her report, casting it in bureaucratic cement.

All the prisoners sitting in the Patrol cars heard Radio trying to raise the troopers to tell them they had the wrong car, wrong license plate. All observed the troopers go right on looking for guns and sniffing drink cups, appearing to ignore the transmissions. All agreed the sergeant was totally unresponsive to the dog owner's fear that it would jump out into the traffic and be killed. Obviously none of this was worth mentioning in a self-justifying police report. Perhaps the thing that hung the sergeant in the end was her final volunteered sentence that "I did not search the women, as I was the on-scene supervisor, overseeing and directing."

Because that statement verified the two women's statements about being groped by a pair of male troopers. Since they were big campaign contributors, the governor was less than amused. The troopers' union also had supported his candidacy but that did not earn them a pass for the reported behavior.

The Seattle *Times* still had old-fashioned reporters then who earned their spurs the hard way and didn't trust cops one damn bit. One of these old dogs interviewed the two couples. Stoked with egalitarian outrage about well-dressed well-to-do women being frisked by male troopers, he sneered at the Patrol's carefully polished reputation for politeness at all costs. Management smarted under his goad--and blamed the sergeant. The good news for twenty-first century abusers of power is that old-fashioned reporters have died out like Tyrannosaurus Rex and manual typewriters.

I'd lay even odds that modern-day idiocies like the Watergate break-in that sank Nixon go unnoticed daily. Citizens (using the term loosely) of this still-new century have been well programmed to dismiss anyone stating a grievance against authority as socially-unbalanced, or just trying to cash in with a big-bucks lawsuit. When an abuse of power tries to break the surface of the technologically-enforced ignorance of the hoi polloi, they can barely be pried from thumbing their communications devices to notice and wonder at the world around them. Spin doctors quickly bowdlerize an issue as raised by some unsavory group whose agenda lacks redeeming social value.

Back in the weary older century, I was all that protected the power structure from the inquiring eye of the dying press. The victims had made a rookie mistake: only slightly gilding the lily (and they may even have believed this) they told *The Times* they were confronted with four big pistols, "drawn and cocked." The reporter believed them, because like almost everybody else he learned his gun-handling by watching TV. Hollywood loves the added drama of cocking revolvers.

Being a kind of primitive spin-doctor, I seized on this minor blunder and told him that if the troopers had cocked the big six-inch Smith & Wesson Model 28s they still carried then, they violated all their training. I explained the Smiths were so well-tuned that double-action was plenty quick and lethal when it came to intentional shooting. I didn't minimize the victims' fears at having a bunch of guns pointed at them in the raining dark. I just said the risk of accidental discharge is magnitudes less when they follow their training. I was quite pedantic; he should go back and check his sources because if they could swear the guns were in fact cocked, they had a legitimate beef.

The silliest things can interrupt a story's momentum. Making a big issue of the cocked-pistol question did it. The victims recanted "cocked." The sergeant's handling of campaign contributors still comprised an embarrassing story. But it only lasted one news cycle and vanished. Not internally, though. The sergeant's career trajectory flattened. That's what happened when you treated people with political juice like ordinary mopes, and compounded it by arguing with them when they didn't like it.

Though of course the brass never described it that way.

"Poor judgment" was the ruling, because she thought she was too important to personally frisk two women in expensive dresses, jewelry and high heels on the side of the road in the rain.

The good news for modern-day functionaries is that given the "wired" world they are unlikely to stub their toe on those who are heavily connected; a modern-day stop would probably have the campaign contributors identified to their last dollar, and to whose treasury it was donated, before anybody waved guns around. The sergeant in charge might even find herself with a tweet from the governor telling her to lay off before she could dig herself a career-damaging hole. But us ordinary mopes better get down in the mud and like it.

A Question of Docket Entries

IN THE LAST DECADE of the last century I heard one of those unsettling stories that haunt you. A young student from the state capital ventured up to the big city. His folks thought nothing of it—he was a good kid, excellent student, well-mannered and not given to wild adventure, so the thought of trouble never crossed their minds.

They never saw him alive again.

The last time they heard from him, he was calling from a jail phone in county jail. They said he was unclear why he had been arrested. With a suspicion never far from the minds of black Americans, they thought it might have been his skin color. But when they got to the big city to see about getting him out, jail officials said they never heard of him. Nope, they said, no records in the computer. He had never been there and he wasn't there now.

The man who told me the story didn't dwell on their confusion and fear or whether they searched the city where they thought their son was going, or went home. He skipped straight to the real heartbreak:

They were called back to the city to identify their son's body.

He had been pulled from the water beneath Aurora Bridge. The medical examiner ruled death by strangulation. There was no water in the boy's lungs, let alone salt water.

A paperback book and other things supposedly found on the floating body were...dry.

The parents did not know or did not tell my informant what the medical examiner decreed as manner of death: suicide, homicide, accident or undetermined. Maybe they did not know the forensic distinction between cause and manner of death. Dead is dead. They buried their son and mourned. My friend was also their friend, and in the dreary aftermath they told him their story. Coming out of numb grief they sought some insight how this could have happened, because their friend had a long and varied law-enforcement administration career.

The gaps in the official story of the death were glaringly evident. But my friend worked for a statewide law-enforcement agency reporting to the governor. A man from that agency questioning county jailors would be viewed by the sheriff as interagency interference. The law enforcement community has iron turf laws. You trespass at your own peril.

Then too, my friend was black. A thorough professional with more than one master's degree in police and public administration, he baldly told me his race would antagonize the sheriff, who would conclude he was just another black troublemaker agitating about a "nowhere" black kid.

Oh, you bet jailors knew the dead boy's parents were not part of the capital power structure. They would have checked that first thing when whatever happened, happened. First question cops ask when things go sideways: is this a grounder or a red ball? Slang varies between departments, but not philosophy: if the victim is connected that requires far different handling than injury to a mere mope.

The boy's parents were not mopes; they were ordinary citizens whose world turned upside down with the mysterious death of their son. No newspaper reported the peculiarities around the boy's death. No political Bigfoot made a phone call to the sheriff. Two thirds of the due diligence indicated this was a grounder. But in the twentieth century the powerless had learned to substitute noise and protest to apply pressure, following Saul Alinsky's *Rules for Radicals*. The peculiar drowning virtually cried out for a demonstration. But there was no public hue and cry. Jail administration probably checked off the third due-diligence box--no black protest--three for three, grounder all the way. Jail personnel went on with life, uninterrupted.

My friend believed his black face asking belated questions would only bury any answers deeper. Now he came to his purpose for telling me the story. One, I was white. Two, he knew my nasal acuity for mendacity. Three, perhaps most important, I was a former newsman with scores of newsroom contacts who would accept my word there was a story here. Could I stir up the Fourth Estate by remote control?

Well yes and no. I made a couple calls to reporters who would not tell the sheriff on me. They concluded the event was too old (a few months) and the jail's story now written in stone. Without inside information, veteran newsies said it was a non-starter, a he-said-they-said with no resolution. I fretted for my lost press card.

I could generate a dozen questions that might peel the stonewall open. Here are a few. What was the official ruling on manner of death? The medical examiner was not a sheriff's patronage employee. How did strangulation, listed as cause, occur with no water in the lungs? Where were the written reports of first responders beneath the bridge? Did they reduce to writing the assertion items taken off the floating body were...dry? How about a public-records search of jail phone records the day he called his parents. Was their number on the long-distance log? Fortunately for the jailors, the parents did not have a phone that captured incoming numbers.

But I had been out of the news business a long time. I was in fact employed by the same police agency as my friend. Therefore I was governed by the same iron interagency protocols. If I shopped the story to too many reporters, word would get back to the sheriff. Reporters supposedly protect their sources at all costs--but I had been burned before.

All these years later the thing still sticks in my craw.

I remember a hoodlum victim of the Tacoma topless-tavern wars in the seventies found floating in a boat basin in Tacoma. The medical report said he drowned, manner of death accidental. *His* lungs were full of water—just not salt water. Bathtub drowning was cause of death; manner was probably suicide. He had threatened the mob he might turn informant. But remembering the good black kid from Olympia for whom no one stood up reminds me of another victim.

Debra Smith did not drown but was autopsied during the Great Flood of Pennsylvania in 1972. The water was receding into the banks of the Susquehanna River after peaking far above the previous high-water mark. I was a reporter then. My newspaper's presses had gone entirely under. Our telephone operator drowned evacuating by small boat. The emergent city stank to high heaven and so did the newspaper building. The good news was that oil scum rode the flood waters up, coating the presses and protecting them from rust. A thorough cleaning and they were good to go.

We were getting back up to speed when the city editor sent me to investigate use of illicit drugs in the county jail. A drug-overdose victim had been brought into Harrisburg Hospital at the height of the flood, dead on arrival, autopsy performed by flashlight because hospital generators were still underwater.

I found a story but not the one he thought I'd find.

Debra Smith was a young black woman found dead in her cell. Just a few hours before she died, an idiotic radio announcer with no shred of journalistic integrity breathlessly told his listeners the dam above county prison was about to break, guards abandoned their posts, and inmates had been left locked up to drown.

At least one prisoner had a transistor radio. Panic ensued.

The lockup was short-staffed all right. Guards couldn't get to work through the same flood that marooned me at home while my newspaper sank. They hadn't abandoned the prison. They never got to work to start with. The dead girl had been a Harrisburg Hospital nurse's aid before she was an inmate. In her short time behind bars she obtained trustee status. The prison's skeleton crew that hectic night relied on her to dole out tranquilizers to terrified prisoners. She reassured them they weren't abandoned and the dam was not breaking. By all accounts she performed well. The crisis passed.

They said they found her collapsed in her cell later, not breathing. When the diagnosis came back drug overdose, prison officials theorized she palmed the fatal dose while calming her fellow inmates.

The huge question was why?

Well, said the prison chaplain, she had just been denied parole. She took that really badly. Her aging parents were going to lose their home without her hospital salary to pay rent. She was their sole means of support.

Why was she denied parole under those circumstances? Was she some kind of hardened criminal? Not at all, the chaplain said—it was her first offense. A terribly tragic story, he added. Tragedy sold newspapers so I started walking back the cat, as the old intelligence hands used to say. Turned out I knew her defense attorney pretty well. His story was hard to credit, but he had never lied to me before.

The tragedy began with this young black nurse's assistant on her way home from work one night. She came upon a street altercation. At its center were two city cops, dragging her bloody boyfriend out of a downtown bar. By her own admission, she rushed through the crowd with one thought: to stop the bleeding. Basic first aid, as anyone who ever trained for combat knows. One of the cops grabbed her. She shoved him away and turned back to her boyfriend. The next thing she knew, she was in cuffs along with her boyfriend, and on the way to jail.

I found the cop who grabbed her and he told me his side of the story: two white cops at a black bar in the middle of the night, breaking up a bar fight and dragging participants out. The black crowd well-lubricated, hostile, not shy about expressing anger at the white pigs. A sudden lunge out of the dark by a black person—he paid no attention to the nurse's whites—and he grabbed her in self-defense. When she shoved him, he had a hot image of the whole crowd collapsing on his partner and him if he didn't act fast.

Cuff 'em, get' em in the car, get the hell out of there; sort things out at the station house. He was maybe more forthcoming than with another reporter because he knew I'd been a military cop. Not Jack Reacher, but I had my moments. Drunken combat engineers treeing a bar to celebrate a completed job could make a hostile Central District mob seem tame when White Hats interfered.

The Harrisburg cops booked the boyfriend for the bar fight and tended to his lacerations. Debra Smith was cited for misdemeanor interference to justify cuffing and transporting her and released on her own recognizance. Clean quick police work in a racially charged era where the situation could have turned ugly. But why was she in county lockup months later when Hurricane Agnes dumped the epic flood on Pennsylvania?

The cop said I'd have to ask the lawyers, or the judge. That question was above his pay grade. Back to the defense attorney; he was bitter. He explained the municipal judge was running for reelection. Racial tensions were high everywhere. So the judge decided to make an example of Debra to show "those people that they can't push our policemen," a direct quote from the bench.

The assistant district attorney told me he didn't want to prosecute her misdemeanor. When Debra's defense attorney suggested deferred prosecution, probation, and no jail time so she could keep her job and look after her folks, he agreed. He formally concurred in the defense petition. But the judge said no dice and threw the book at her: maximum months he could impose for a first misdemeanor. He handily won reelection.

The months dragged by. Just before Hurricane Agnes came to town, Debra was up for her first parole hearing. The DA told me he once again formally joined the defense petition to grant it. After all, he remarked, the election was over. But again the judge said no dice. Her folks were evicted for non-payment of rent. All the furniture she purchased for them was put in the street.

So she killed herself.

It wasn't the story the city editor sent me to get. But it was still quite a story. It stirred up the readership. The judge's daughter wrote a passionate letter to the paper, in effect disowning her father. The Black Panthers spray-painted graffiti on the courthouse walls, asking, "Who killed Debra Smith?" The judge was not pleased.

My executive editor was the judge's country club golf and poker buddy. A couple of weeks after the story ran, the judge handed him what purported to be the transcript of the woman's trial. It was typed up and attested by a court clerk who owed her job to the judge's patronage. This alleged transcript was what H.G. Mencken in his Baltimore newspaper days called a "howler," which is to say an official lie. It quoted one of the arresting cops as saying Debra kicked him so hard in the groin he collapsed and lost hold of her boyfriend, who escaped and was still at large.

The cop whose quotes I had in my notebook, and in my story, suddenly would not return my calls. The defense attorney furiously said for publication the transcript was bogus; there was no such testimony. The boyfriend hadn't escaped. He was jailed and charged, paid his fine for fighting and was released. Nor had Debra ever been charged with aiding a prisoner to escape, a more serious crime than misdemeanor interference.

When I called the assistant DA to discuss the putative transcript, he professed a poor memory as to what was said at trial. He did not recant what he told me the first time. But he declined to contradict the allegations in the transcript. He was in a fix with the judge for his published remarks, so I didn't press him about undercharging if Debra really assaulted the cop and aided her boyfriend's escape.

I did say the defense guy is a member of the bar. He is on record calling the transcript bogus. Serious misconduct if he is lying, so what sanctions do the judge and bar contemplate? The DA chuckled. That's not how things are done. The judge will punish him on some other case, and some poor schmuck will never know what hit him. If you need a lawyer anytime soon, don't hire him! He thought I might need one because the judge wanted me fired.

If not for my membership in the newspaper guild and its steward, my cynical city editor, I would have been a goner. Instead I found myself in a tense meeting with editors from the executive editor on down. Mr. Doran was quietly furious about the public humiliation of his country club pal. But he had sent me on controversial stories himself, and approved others I broke; he knew my track record. Without quite knowing how, the feature writer had become their go-to investigative reporter.

I told him I stood by my notes. He nodded grudging acceptance. And oh yeah, I said – here's a photocopy of the docket sheet showing her boyfriend was in fact booked into city jail the night of the incident. I had asked the cop-shop reporter to obtain it before the story ran; part of a reporter's routine due diligence.

There was a long, freighted silence. The executive editor weighed the docket sheet photocopy in one hand and the bogus transcript in the other. Then the meeting was adjourned with no further comment. Getting the docket sheet was routine; I had no crystal ball that a sitting judge would lie on paper to rewrite history in what purported to be an official court transcript. That's how naïve I was the summer before Nixon's landslide election victory and the drumroll of Watergate revelations that followed.

The link in my mind between Debra Smith and the boy found decades later, strangled without water in his lungs below the Aurora Bridge? It is the question of docket entries. You book suspects via computer now – there is no paper arrest docket in the public lobby open for all to view. For a long time in the United States it was a given that people with badges had to be held accountable for what they did with people in custody. A paper docket in public view, entered in ink, established where an arrested individual was held. It was a lot harder to falsify than a computer entry.

The boy told his parents he had been arrested, no reason articulated. Back in the day the docket entry would have specified the reason as that one did that vindicated my Debra Smith story. Probably so would a computer entry on the screen replacing paper dockets. But there was no such entry – at least according to the deputies with access to that screen. No evidence the boy had ever been in custody.

Just for the sake of argument let's suppose the boy told

his parents the truth: he was in jail, allowed his phone call. Now, say something bad happened. It was sadly common back then for suspects arguing about being arrested to be viewed as "non-compliant." Code for let's rough the mope up. A favorite tactic was the much-loved police choke-hold, a procedure that requires finesse and good judgment. Say the chokehold goes awry. The prisoner is strangled to death. Nobody meant that to happen. You sure wish it hadn't. What a damned unfortunate mess.

Time for the evaluation: was the victim's family connected? Were they black activists? Likely to call a newspaper? But wait! A few key strokes can "vanish" him from jail as quickly as southern republic hemisphere banana republics vanish dissidents. Sliding the body off the dock below the Aurora Bridge is chancier, so make the careless choker do it. And he will owe the administration big-time. Wait for the floater to be reported and go on with life. Oh, you're talking about that poor kid who probably jumped off the Aurora Bridge? Nope, never heard of him; certainly never had him in custody here.

There is no paper docket in a public lobby. The computer docket in the machine controlled by jailors behind bulletproof glass is clean as a whistle, even if someone could access it. No trace of a young black man from the state capital there. In today's paperless world I suspect an electronic entry proving Debra Smith's boyfriend was booked and jailed would be replaced by a report he escaped and was still at large, confirming the bogus court transcript.

No wonder reporters I talked to about the strangled young man said there was no way into the story. I don't envy reporters today trying to uncover facts. The computer age has made the truth more malleable than even Orwell envisioned. It depends on who last had the keyboard. Supposedly there are forensic applications that can track and retrieve deletions. But reporters are not furnished such electronic gear. Let alone grieving parents.

The Ethics of Forensic Science

THERE IS AN amazing amount of politicking that goes on behind the scenes in law-enforcement. For almost a decade I worked where there were constant machinations to seize control of the state crime lab, for instance. The lab reposed within the state police structure, and other agencies were not beyond maneuvering behind the scenes to take it over. No agency willingly surrenders its divisions to another, so the fight was on.

The struggle most often played out in the corridors of the Legislature, with hearings and testimony and plenty of lobbying outside the public eye. Complaints about alleged mismanagement of backlogs and such occasionally would make it into the news, particularly if there was a hot case somewhere.

One of the deputy chiefs whose duties included oversight of the crime lab was a subtle man. He instructed lab techs to compile reports showing when they were unswayed by pressure from an arresting agency or a prosecuting attorney, and developed proof of a suspect's innocence. He had these included with cases where the forensics established irrefutable evidence of guilt. The point he wished to emphasis was that forensics was science, and forensics specialists were best employed by a statewide agency that enabled them to work for a scientific result without fear or favor. His compilation provided me excellent fodder to show reporters when the struggle for crime lab control went public. I don't know how much his work influenced the final legislative decision to leave the lab where it was, but the effort to strip it away never made it out of committee. What impressed me more than his subtle approach was the man's personal ethics: he absolutely believed his argument that forensics must follow the truth wherever it led.

Another utterly ethical public servant I was privileged to know in those days was the man who supervised investigations by the state Public Disclosure Commission. A retired Army officer of the best type who had served in Vietnam as a military advisor long before the Johnson years of massive buildup and war, he was a good raconteur: South Vietnam still was largely undemolished when he was there and he told of close encounters with Bengal tigers on patrol. He carried a Springfield .30-06 bolt-action rifle because tigers seemed more a threat than VC. He thought about sending home for some 220-grain hunting loads for a tiger hunt but didn't think it proper to use his privileged status to collect a trophy when civilians no longer had the opportunity. We came to know each other during a long investigation involving official corruption, organized crime and a mob-purchased sheriff when I was with the Liquor Control Board. When all that ran its course we met occasionally for pleasant lunches and yarn-spinning.

The paths of the ethical deputy chief who oversaw the crime lab and the ethical public disclosure official intersected when the latter called me to ask if he could refer a relative to me for information about the crime lab. His relative was a public defender in the State of Alaska who had read a wire-service story quoting me about the impeccable work of the state crime lab in establishing innocence as well as guilt. He wanted to verify this was in fact the philosophy of the crime lab story personally. The story he had seen was about a rape case. The suspect was already in custody of a sheriff's office when told his handwriting matched a threatening note found on the rape victim's car after the assault. Not only was it his handwriting, it demonstrated guilty knowledge of the crime. The arresting deputy recognized him from a composite sketch approved by the victim. The deputy developed the suspect's name and address though licensing records. He grew so violent in his fury at being arrested that the courts denied bail. Then the victim identified him in a lineup. The case appeared to be a slam dunk. But his defense attorney believed his client's innocence and pressured the authorities to have the state crime lab examine the evidence.

The state document examiner reviewed the incriminating note against hand-writing exemplars of the accused rapist. He asked for and got exemplars from the alleged victim. He found no similarities between the suspect's handwriting and the post-assault note. He described a strong probability the note was written by the alleged victim. When confronted with the forensics, the woman not only admitted she wrote the note, she admitted she had invented the rape. Charges were dropped. The innocent man went free—after four months in jail due to his rightful anger at being arrested for something he never did, and to flawed handwriting analysis by the sheriff's office.

My friend's relative, the public defender in Alaska, had

not enjoyed the same cooperation from our crime lab. Police accused his client of shooting at them, and had him for attempted murder. The public defender contacted one of our state's ballistics experts vacationing in Anchorage and asked him to examine shooting evidence obtained in discovery. The vacationing firearms specialist was a court-approved expert in anything ballistic you could name. In the arcane world of forensics, he was a star. He applied his usual methods to the Alaska evidence. He concluded the alleged ambush shooting could not have happened the way the police said; physics did not support the charging narrative.

The Alaska prosecutor and the cops were furious. The tech's credentials were unassailable. If his testimony was allowed to come in, their shooting evidence would be thrown out. The scenario put forward by the cops would collapse, followed by the entire prosecution. Trial was scheduled. The firearms tech promised to take annual leave if the public defender's office footed his return flight to Alaska to testify. The defense attorney thought he'd won. He was very happy the news story about our crime lab's rigorous objectivity in the alleged rape, which inspired him to seek out the ballistics tech, had proved true.

Then our tech changed his mind.

He wouldn't testify after all. Almost as if he had prior notice of that decision, the prosecutor immediately moved the court to exclude preliminary ballistic findings, absent the tech's live testimony. The blindsided public defender called the tech to plead with him to testify. But the tech was cowed. It would be worth his job and pension to testify in Alaska. No, he wasn't just paranoid. He had been told the consequences in no uncertain terms by his direct superior, a uniformed captain.

Lawyers don't like being blindsided any more than anyone. So the public defender called his uncle the top investigator of corruptions at the Public Disclosure Commission. He had relied on our statement of ethics in forensics science that we used to fend of hostile takeover of the crime lab by other agencies. He could comprehend no scientific distinction between objective study of handwriting exemplars and objective study of ballistics. Since I was in the story asserting this lofty standard upon which he had relied, he asked my PDC friend to call me. My friend said in fifteen years of public service together he had never known me to willing make false statements to the media. But our crime-lab forensics didn't seem as ethical in practice as I (and the chief and the deputy chief who drew up the philosophy) said. I had a dreadful sinking feeling.

I had not been aware that particular captain had been shuffled into the crime lab. The state patrol had a quaint custom of installing commissioned troopers as commanders over every single division, civilian or not. In the case of the much-contested crime lab, it didn't matter that its civilian director held varying advanced degrees and had enjoyed a long and distinguished national forensics career and recruited the best. All well and good, Doctor, but you still must get your operation approved by a guy with a badge and gun.

From the moment troopers completed their obligatory four years on the road, the ambitious ones maneuvered for these soft office jobs. Troopers anointed captain were patronage employees serving at the pleasure of the chief.

They couldn't be fired for displeasing that personage but they could be bumped back to their last merit rank. I know of grown men including a tough SWAT commander who openly cried when a new chief demoted them. The perks of rank are addictive. But the present situation was odd. My chief had set the policy for strict scientific ethics in forensics as laid out by the ethical old deputy chief who oversaw the crime lab and all detectives before he retired.

Would a newly shuffled in captain working for a new deputy chief who already had his foot half out the door, having been recruited for police chief of a midsize city? Could the captain be positioning himself for job security by currying favor with outsiders who would return the favor and speak to the new chief on his behalf? Would he actually bypass the august civilian crime lab director to lean directly on a forensics tech?

Of course he would. I knew this captain's record: he had rotated through personnel, fiscal and other administrative functions. His bureaucratic record was as unblemished as his tailored uniforms and he presented the bland friendly face of a classic road trooper helping you change a flat tire. He was a known team player and played by the rules; all the rules, written and unwritten. He really wasn't happy when I called for an explanation.

He blandly confirmed to me the Alaska prosecutor contacted him to demand he call off his ballistics expert. Confirmed that he directed the tech not to testify about his forensic findings in Alaska. Further, he directed in writing that the firearms tech--and by extension the rest of the crime lab--were *never* to testify where that testimony contradicted any other law enforcement agency. He wrote the Alaska prosecutor to promise no one under his command would do so. He had been in personnel when the innocent man was freed of bogus rape charges leveled by a sheriff's office.)

This captain was low-key, courteous, usually an accessible sort of guy and understood that I had the ear of the chief. He understood I was on the hook for public pronouncements that his new orders made a lie. He approved of the PR that helped beat back a hostile takeover of the lab. But this was police business now. He tightened right up when I said I am not in the habit of lying to the public and I don't like being put in that barrel, He absolutely could see no issue. The PR did its job and now he was doing his. He carried a badge. I didn't. If I didn't understand that bright line, I was myself suspect.

His attitude was implacable as McCarthy finding Reds in the State Department. Forensics existed to prove cops' cases were righteous, period. The tech should never have agreed to evaluate evidence on behalf of a defense attorney. For doing so he had been labeled a troublemaker. The captain flatly confirmed the tech's job was on the line; he also would direct the patrols' assistant attorney general to resist an Alaska defense subpoena. His very strong implication was that if I rocked the boat I would also be a troublemaker. My absolute access to my chief stopped him short of an open declaration.

The deputy chief whose ethics I admired had retired. I got along fine with his successor, the future city police chief, who was politically astute. He was also a fresh-minted attorney. I wanted to put him together with my PDC friend for a discussion of forensic ethics. My friend demurred. He was disappointed to see the agency's public stance on forensics was a lie. But he worried it would be improper to bring outside pressure because a relative of his had relied on that lie and was burned--never mind the Alaska suspect the forensics had cleared. He would spread word in the legal community that disinterested crime-scene analysis was just a PR stunt. Knowing the defense bar view of cops they wouldn't bat an eye.

The science was plain: the Alaska forensics either supported the cops, or didn't. Anything else was official corruption. But since no one had been paid off the PDC would not be officially involved. It's the way corruption really works--a slow seepage of understandings, one hand washing the other.

My old reporter's instincts were highly agitated. I imagined a nationwide conspiracy of forensics silence to protect wrong-doing by cops—a sure Pulitzer for the reporter who could prove it. But I hadn't been a reporter in a long time. My chief was set to retire, a new governor to whom ethics was a joke was about to be seated, and there are some battles you just can't win. I don't know what happened to the guy in an Alaska jail. I do know I cannot bring myself to watch all those TV forensics dramas about how heroic and objective crime labs are. They turn my stomach.

Nervous Times

"THOSE WERE nervous times," Art said. He gnawed the stem of his reading glasses and peered at me above stacks of legal documents on his desk. "We didn't know if he was going to make it."

I had stepped around the corner from my office to talk to our senior assistant attorney general about impending seizure of a semi-load of bootleg liquor bound for an Indian reservation outside Seattle. The operation was being run out of our Tacoma office. Art was talking about the man heading it up, who had been gunned down in front of his family before I went to work for the Liquor Control Board.

The man himself had described that day to me: backing his state car out of the garage, two men walking swiftly toward him, the gunfire almost before he registered their presence. He absorbed several hits from a .32 in his left shoulder, after the slugs penetrated the car door. But the guy with the sawed-off shotgun missed his whole car, taking out window glass in a house across the street. Our liquor cop curled down into a ball on the floorboards, his James Bond Walther PPK belatedly in his hand and cocked, peering up at the windows, hoping to fight back if they closed in for a kill shot. It seemed to take a long time to realize they weren't coming and that he was hearing a siren in the street. The last thing he remembered was carefully uncocking his PPK.

He was lucky that day in so many ways. He was a big guy, almost my size, and in good health for starters. A .32 is a pipsqueak cartridge and the rounds peeled off a lot of velocity going through in the door. One bullet got through his arm and reached his heart--and stopped there, barely nudging without penetrating. The shotgunner who couldn't shoot straight missed him altogether. Luckiest of all, an ambulance was in the next block on a heart-attack call. The attendants heard the shots and were with him in minutes.

Recovery still took a long time. Real people don't shake off gunshot wounds like they do in the movies. He lost a lot of weight. He still didn't have full strength in his left arm when he went back to work. The shooters were long gone and their trail was cold. For all its ineptitude, it had clearly been a hit. Suspicion centered on hoodlums warring for control of the Tacoma topless-tavern business. There had been tavern arsons and mysterious deaths—a man found drowned in a salt-water estuary with no salt water in his lungs was one memorable one.

That's where things stood the autumn I left one of the best jobs I ever had, in Arizona with the Game and Fish Department, and moved back to Washington to take over public relations for the Liquor Control Board, an agency created the year they repealed Prohibition. It was my first job for an agency viewed with such constant hostility by the press, including the U.S. Navy during the Vietnam War. Two of the sitting board members and a retired former chairman were fighting an indictment for misuse of government funds involving vast private gifts of liquor that predated my arrival. Large corporate interests periodically attempted to "take the state out of the business" of selling liquor so grocery stores and the like could make that money instead of the state treasury. A lot of accusations floated about favoritism in granting of liquor licenses. And there were the topless-tavern wars.

Almost as soon as I took the job, Indian tribes joined the fun, selling untaxed liquor on their reservations. We'd had agents in Oklahoma investigating companies that sold to the tribes. They developed intelligence that would lead to shipment seizures before the booze made it to the reservations. Art, our staff attorney general, had been there for it all and was reminiscing.

"Nervous times," he said again. In his tweed sport coat with his graying hair brushed back neatly, hunched in a perennial desk man's stoop above his papers, he resembled nothing so much as a benevolent college professor you would expect to be nervous about attempted assassinations.

It took some imagination to envision an Army Air Force cap with a fifty-mission crush perched on his younger head, Art in the left seat of a bomber, flying repeatedly through flak above the Ploesti oil wells. They lost two engines on the same side on one mission and he had to get them home, essentially dangling sideways from the other two, and figure out some pilot's trick to level off for landing, and he did. Not the kind of guy to get nervous easily.

"Every time I walked out to my car," he told me, "I would start thinking about things. And I'd pop the hood and check around a little. The mob tends to like car bombs, you realize."

We discussed what to tell the media once we had the bootleg Indian shipment in hand. We agreed our agent who had been wounded should take the lead when cameras showed up. The media already knew him from his survival story. I would brief him on what he could and couldn't say. It was late afternoon when I got the call his men had seized the truck without incident and the liquor was being inventoried. Our recovering gunshot victim told me to go ahead and notify the media that he would be standing by at our liquor warehouse for sound bites.

When I began my notification of assignment desks, it was the second or third station I called when, well into my spiel I noticed the silence emanating from the phone. "You still there?" I said.

"You do realize, don't you, that the Sheriff of Pierce County was arrested tonight by federal agents?" was the surprising answer.

"Why would I know that?"

"Are you serious? He's being charged with hiring the hit on your guy, the guy you're sending us to see right now." The TV guy was getting excited. "Did you know the Feds interviewed your guy last night?"

I admitted I did not know that.

"They read him his rights first. You know what that means don't you?"

"Wait – read who his rights?"

"Your guy that was shot! They must have thought he was dirty."

Jesus H. Christ on a tricycle – Arizona's uncontroversial desert looked pretty good just then. The assignments editor rang off, but not before I heard him yell to get a crew rolling toward our warehouse where our suspect liquor inspector was waiting. I called the warehouse and got our guy on the line. He had been informed of the sheriff's arrest. But not that the media was looking at him as dirty. Hell, he was the victim! He didn't want his textbook-clean seizure of Indian liquor lost in leading questions about all that. Neither did I.

I told him you need to leave right now, because you have received word of another truckload on the way in and you need to investigate.

"I have?" Nervous chuckle. "I do?"

'You have," I said. "I just informed you. Get the hell out of there. Let your second-in-command deal with the media on the Indian liquor."

That's the way it went down. The media didn't like it much. I was on the phone half the night fielding squawks of outrage because they couldn't find our guy to ask about the sheriff. After a couple calls I had my self-righteous reply down pat: liquor enforcement against tribes couldn't just stop because the media wanted an interview. Seizure of untaxed liquor by the semi-truck load was a big deal. Plus I wasn't even here when that mob stuff was happening, so you'll just have to cool your heels.

We got the coverage we wanted on the liquor seizure. The chairman of the Liquor Board sent me to Tacoma next day and run interference. The story about the bent sheriff was heating up, rumors the shooters had been arrested in Bangkok and faced extradition, that they were hired in Kansas City on behalf of the sheriff and rented their guns from a mob armorer there--and returned them! Reporters were telling me more than I was telling them and it was a frenetic morning.

When lunch time rolled around several of the liquor cops loaded into one of the official sedans and sneaked off to a restaurant not frequented by the media. I was seated to the left of our wounded warrior in the back seat with a beefy liquor agent on his other side and two more up front. He examined the seating arrangements with satisfaction.

"Thanks," he said. "They'll have to throw a lot of lead to get through you guys before they get me." The other guys chuckled. I was the only unarmed one.

"What the hell are you talking about?" I said.

"Well, the Feds told me I'm their star witness now," he said. "The bad boys won't like that."

Jesus H. Christ on a motorcycle. Why had I ever left Arizona?

Nervous times, Art said the day before, and nervous times they still were. These guys, for all their chuckles, were nervous. I was nervous. The man of the hour was trying to put a macho face on it, but he was more nervous than any of us. No damn wonder. When we got back to the office, we stood around in the parking lot keeping an eye out while he got in his car, which he had backed in. He said he even backed it into his garage now – he never was going to back out into the street or out of a parking space again. Who could blame him?

He left for a spot he thought was safe, where his family was sequestered; we all agreed he should. When the Tacoma office closed for the day, the media was just getting into full cry as they uncovered more about the sheriff's involvement in the topless-tavern war. Everybody wanted comments from the Liquor Control Board. That meant me. When the last armed enforcement officer left for the day, I went out to my pickup truck and got my own gun from behind the seat. This office was in the crosshairs and I was now its sole occupant.

In Arizona, you could carry a pistol openly just about

anywhere. My sidearm of choice was a Ruger single-action .45 with a 7 1/2 – inch barrel, a cowboy pistol. Back in Washington, I found a generic Mexican steer-hide shoulder rig. I couldn't afford Bianchi Leather. I was big enough to tuck the big pistol under my arm without anybody noticing. Max Brand always wrote that the draw from a shoulder holster was faster than from the belt. Firearms experts disagreed, but I went with Max Brand.

The night wore on in repeated interviews. I was getting hoarse. The office coffee smelled burned and tasted worse. I found myself reared back in a chair with my feet on the desk, rattling off answers on automatic pilot.

Somebody bashed in the door so hard it slammed against the wall.

I was on my feet facing the door with the Ruger at full-cock in less time than it takes to tell it.

"Por Dios!" The janitor had slammed the door open with his back because his hands were full of cleaning supplies. Stuff hit the floor, spilling cleanser. He damn near fainted. His hands shot up. Over the Ruger's sights, his face was as pale as the soap powder on the floor.

"Sorry!" I said.

But I walked to the door and looked out, just to be sure. Then I uncocked the Ruger and put it away, pulled in his wheeled mop bucket, and helped him clean up the spill— after I made sure the door was locked behind us. Meanwhile I was mentally thanking my long-dead grandfather for the rigid firearms discipline he instilled from age four: never shoot until you're sure of your target.

Nervous times indeed.

Two Orphan Chapters from *Newspaper Gypsy*

Dry Sunday

THE CHRONICLE WAS A MORNING NEWSPAPER, so Eddy Miller worked nightside, which suited him just fine. He covered city hall and county government because it was easier for him than selling washing machines for Sears, Roebuck in Charleston, or learning address schemes at the Post Office in Savannah. He made more money on commission at Sears and had more job security at the Post Office, but this was easier. No pressure to meet sales quotas; no bureaucratic hassles from ex-military assholes who had seniority in the federal service.

As for actual newspaper work, he really didn't have a good reporter's eye or a gift of language, but he could string sentences together in the standard news format and never argued with copy editors who wanted to change his stuff. He had more or less stumbled into the newspaper business when his old Mercury blew a head gasket in Augusta on his way to Atlanta after he quit the Post Office. He'd had money enough to drive to California, which is where he was going, but not if he had to have a complete engine rebuild first.

So he answered an ad in the Chronicle for a sports reporter, figuring how hard could it be, given his knowledge and love of all sports. He bs'ed the personnel manager, quoting Sally League baseball statistics and citing famous college football games he had seen, selling himself like a Kenmore refrigerator, and sliding right past the usual job requirement for a portfolio of news clippings. Then he leveled with the sports editor about his snow job in personnel, recited his knowledge of all team sports, and stuck long enough to write publishable stories.

Eddy was nothing if not a talker, and he actually had been a Rotarian and a Lion in his previous lives, so he got on well with small-town business people and city employees. In six months, he knew his way around pretty well and was popular in the newsroom, and the city editor was a drinking buddy. Before too long his buddy talked him into giving straight news a try and here he was getting to know all the ins and outs of small city moving and shaking.

He got his Mercury fixed, and kept thinking that when he got a new stake built up he would load up his car and head west again. But he had developed a pretty enviable string of female admirers by then, randy Southern belles with a weakness for a line of patter and a knowing hand, and here he was, still.

But God, he hated dry Sundays.

There was slang then to the effect that any place interesting or exciting was "where it's at." The limit of Eddy's sensitivity was to know that a dry Sunday in Georgia wasn't where it was, and never was going to be. Sunday was dry because the governor of Georgia that year was a Baptist deacon who had entered journalistic history as a restaurateur who chased Negroes who tried to sit in his restaurant with a hickory ax handle. Once elected to statewide office, the deacon went after Sunday drinkers with Prohibitionist fervor, wielding an executive order like he had wielded his trademark anti-integration tool.

On dry Sundays, Eddy was reduced to doing his dirty laundry at the Laundromat on Walton Way. At two-thirty a.m. this Monday after another interminable dry Sunday, he had the place to himself except for a woman who looked like a sub-moron with a filthy kid clinging to her worn print dress. The kid looked like a refugee in one of those TV commercials about the Third World. The Laundromat was better than his apartment, even with a half-full bottle of Jack Daniel's in the cupboard and a six-pack of beer he kept in the refrigerator in case anybody ever stopped by. Once in a while somebody did. But whiskey was hateful stuff when he was drinking alone and beer made him sick to his stomach drinking it in an empty apartment.

Eddy had never been drunk or sick after drinking in bars. He loved to drink in bars, even beer, and by now he knew all the spots and the night people even a small city this size supported. He was quite a social drinker on a normal night. Nobody bothered him on the desk about taking a drink or three as he made his rounds; night council meetings and civic club dinners and political rallies always had booze on hand. Drinking was an accepted and even expected part of his work, just like it had been on the sports beat.

He was quite a social drinker all right. It was almost a job qualification. And he had time after the final deadline to hit a few spots on his own hook, maybe buy a round at the Magnolia Club where the other news guys hung out unless he had scored a new woman. Then he'd go dance a dance or two and get laid at her place or some convenient motel. Either way, he could then float on home to bed in a pleasant alcoholic haze. He could sleep, then, really sleep if he'd scored; and when he woke up it would be safely noontime and he would be fine, fresh and ready for the day. But early Monday after a dry Sunday was just awful.

His wash was just soaping up good when a beat-up Chevrolet pickup rolled in. One headlight was out. The black couple in it brought in five baskets of dirty laundry and the Sunday paper. The man was ratty and smelled of dirty automobile engines. The woman was sleazy and sexless, and her grimy slip showed six inches beneath her dress hem all around. Nobody spoke or looked at each other. It was pretty grim, but still better than the apartment alone with the undrinkable booze and the unsleepable bed.

When he was alone at the apartment and cold sober, he could hear his mother in his head, telling him to go to bed. It was his strongest memory of her, always telling him go to bed, go to bed, tomorrow comes mighty early. Just close your eyes and you'll be asleep. But he never was, even as a youth. He had been wide-awake for hours listening to everybody else sleep. Sometimes he imagined that the Creature from the Black Lagoon, The Thing, or some other horror from the movies was creeping through the night, zeroing in on his house, and would get him if he dared to close his eyes. He always did close his eyes eventually and the creatures never came and got him, but the next night would be the same until his memory of that particular movie faded. Terrified or not, his main childhood memory was nights awake listening to the family sleep.

Now he didn't even have anybody sleeping to listen to, and he hated going to bed worse than ever. Which was why he found the night newspaper work so easy. You couldn't sell washing machines or deliver mail at night, but you could go to political fish fries out on the levee or cover county council hearings and listen to angry citizens raise hell about the roads. Then you could drink until the bars closed. If he was in a certain frame of mind, and he often was, he could go across the river to South Carolina and hit a couple of the unlicensed bottle clubs that never closed till dawn. But a lot of those clubs closed on Sundays too, not wanting to tempt fate and the beverage control cops. So dry Sundays he was stuck. When he tried to go to bed cold sober, the apartment was so quiet his ears rang. His ears invented sounds: somebody touching the toilet handle, that little clink just before the explosion of the flush; or the slither of a toothbrush being taken out of its holder beside the mirror. He would lie there not really asleep and not really awake and, just for a moment, think he was not alone. Then he would open his eyes and the silence would unload on him, ears ringing as if he'd fired a gun in a closed space.

He had left his wife behind in Charleston. Just got up one day and packed his things while she was at the hairdresser's and loaded up his two-year-old Buick Roadmaster. He signed his Cadillac that he'd bought with appliance commissions over to her and left the paperwork on the nightstand by the bed. Then he drove the Buick down to a car dealer he played poker with and traded it for the old Mercury and cash back, and shifted his stuff into the Merc. When he went back to tell his wife that he was leaving, she said I hope you're happy with that slut and shut the door in his face.

He drove down to Savannah that night though his Post Office reporting date wasn't for two weeks; and moved in with Gail. She called those two weeks their honeymoon, swimming at Tybee Beach, dancing in the beach clubs and making out on the sand and in the back of the old Mercury. Maybe he should have changed apartments after Gail left him. Maybe that's what he should have done. She had been up for the grand road trip across America as he described it, but not for being stuck in Augusta. She left him as soon as she realized that he was settling in. Almost before he realized it himself.

It was as if she left ghosts of the little domestic sounds she used to make when she was around the place, just to haunt him. That seemed a silly thing for a grown man to think, but he still thought it. Especially in the wee hours of a dry Sunday when he was cold sober and the other side of the bed was empty and cold. He never brought his girl friends home. Maybe that would have cleared the air and chased away the imagined sounds, but he just didn't do it.

When Gail ditched him, all the other reporters and most of his new bar friends agreed that he should have just thrown all her belongings in the trash. But he hadn't done that. He had lived with their silent reproach until she wrote where she wanted them sent in Savannah. Then he packed everything up in six cheap tin trunks and sent the trunks to her on the Greyhound. All except her iced-tea pitcher and glasses in the cupboard. He never looked in cupboards when he was by himself, so he missed them. When the reading lamp by the bed went bad and he was looking for a place to stuff it so he wouldn't keep trying to turn it on, he found the tea pitcher and glasses. She was back with her husband by then, all her wild oats evidently sown. It would have been pretty awkward for her to explain a package of dishes mailed from Augusta. But he still felt bad about overlooking them. They probably weren't among her favorite things or she would have written to ask about them long before now. But he felt bad just the same.

His wash had finished its cycle now. He transferred it to a dryer. None of the others in the Laundromat looked at him or said anything. But he could feel them watching him. Looking at what he was washing. He could feel their eyes on the back of his neck. When the dryer started, he walked to the plate glass window across the front. There were old cigarette decals on it. There was another ancient decal, partly scraped away, but you could still read "White Only."

The only time Gail ever came here with him, she thought the sign meant no colored fabrics could be washed. Gail was so Southern it never would have occurred to her that you had to post a decal to keep Negroes out of a Laundromat in the white part of town. By the time they were there, the right of Negroes to wash their clothes in a Laundromat of their choosing had already been established, even in Georgia, so she hadn't made the connection until he explained it. She heaved a sigh and said "all gone with the wind." He didn't know what she meant, but that was Gail for you.

Outside Eddy could see, but not hear or feel, the wind blowing. Trash, leaves, pages of a discarded newspaper, probably the Chronicle. He stepped outside to feel and hear the wind. A dog that had been trotting along the side of the building stopped short, dropped its ears and slunk off across the street, watching him over its tail. Dogs never were much good at pretending when they were someplace they weren't supposed to be. The filling station across the street looked modern as a science-fiction story, but one of its signs squeaked in the wind like a rusty gate.

Eddy wondered where all the night people went after the bars closed Saturday at midnight. Midnight! That crazed deacon had to be voted out. They all agreed on that anyway; the cocktail waitresses in their black mesh stockings, the pool hustlers, the also-ran band members in their tarnished show clothes and the female barflies who began to look pretty good before the lights came up at closing time. But he doubted if a single one of them was even registered to vote. Neither was he. He was going to have to do something about that before some politician checked the rolls on him.

The night people would start to show up again Monday night as the bars reopened. By Wednesday they all would be accounted for. But where were they tonight? What were they doing instead of straggling out of bars that closed at two-thirty on a normal night, headed out for breakfast at the Busy Bee or the Huddle House? He had never seen a single night person on Sunday since this one-day Prohibition set in. And he had looked too; driving all the way out Broad Street to East Boundary, then back up Walton Way past the Partridge Inn and the rich peoples' homes, then across Monte Sano past the sad dark abandoned-looking Tip Top Cafe. Eddy never had the nerve to ask where they went. He couldn't believe they all went across the river to crowd into the one or two clubs that stayed open on Sunday because they had the fix in with the right authorities.

Eddy really would have liked to go back to those clubs himself, but it was no longer safe for him. He'd wound up sleeping with the current girl friend of the half-crazy Greek owner of those two clubs who, when he was depressed, would shoot holes in the ceiling with a big nickel-plated .44 revolver to let people know the show was over for that night.

Eddy had only escaped a bad beating or worse because he was a Chronicle reporter and the Chronicle was a force to be reckoned with on both sides of the river. If the newspaper turned up the heat on the South Carolina beverage authorities, the Greek's Sunday protection would evaporate and he'd lose a bundle. One of the Greek's redneck bouncers, an ex-Gamecock linebacker, had been delegated to explain this to Eddy and take away his member key. He was no longer welcome. The hell of it was she hadn't been that good in the sack.

But he couldn't believe the Greek got all the night people on Sunday. He did not like to pry, which was a lousy attitude for a reporter. Perhaps more, he didn't want to seem pathetic, asking about a place he was not welcome or seeming to angle for an invitation to some private get-together at somebody's home. He believed that the night people accepted him. They even used the nickname his newspaper cronies had bestowed on him, Lightnin' Man, for his way with the lonely ladies of the night. He was good for a tab at more than just the Magnolia Club, where all the newsies ran one. He got free drinks a good bit, because he was the nightside news guy who covered politics—a good contact.

The night people followed sports reports like bulletins from a war zone, and always thought he knew the inside scoop because he started as a sports reporter. He got invited to all the low-ante poker games, and even a couple where the stakes were a little rich, because they knew he also played poker with the county commissioners and the mayor. The small-time bookies always gave him the line to bet on the college and pro cards, and were so accurate that he made a nice little supplement to his salary and poker winnings that way. The gamblers were intensely interested in all sports, even local high school sports, and seemed to know an awful lot about which team was healthy and likely to win. He supposed there might be a story in there somewhere about gamblers having some much inside knowledge; there had to be a fix in somewhere. A real reporter's nose would have been twitching, but Eddy didn't pry. His main curiosity was where they all went after early bar closing on Saturday and where they stayed until Monday night.

He put his folded dry clothing in the clean white laundry sack that he always washed with the clothing. It had been olive drab when it was issued to him in Basic Training. He thought it was the only enduring thing the Army had ever given him. There was a 24-hour Huddle House down the street. Eddy locked his laundry in the Mercury and walked down there and ordered a breakfast steak with grits and coffee. He was the only customer. After the waitress asked him what he wanted, she never spoke again, not even to say good night. She had pale, uncommunicative eyes, which looked as if they were accustomed to total silence and preferred it. So he didn't play the jukebox, or try to talk to her. He wondered if she missed the night people who would be here tomorrow morning about this time after the bars closed. She didn't look as if she missed anybody.

He ate fast and mechanically, and paid his check in silence except for the ding of the cash register. The food was warm and heavy and irrelevant in his stomach as he went back out into the windy night and got into his car. He hadn't even been hungry; he was just putting off going home sober as long as he could. He drove up Walton Way. It was three forty-five by the bank clock on the corner. Another dry Sunday survived. He was so glad that it was finally and irrevocably Monday that he almost felt like waiting up to watch the sun rise, just to be sure.

Charlie Whitesox

ALL THE REGULARS from the nightside Chronicle staff were at their usual table in the Magnolia Club when Charlie Brown came in out of the raining night. The first thing Charlie heard, as he handed his crisp new London Fog trench coat and sodden felt hat to the Negro doorman, was Calhoun's loud mouth. Calhoun was the night news editor and sometimes temporary managing editor during the periodic purges staged by the executive editor, who tended to fire hotshot editors when they were so good that he felt threatened. They had a new managing editor again, from North Carolina, and his honeymoon with the man upstairs still had not run its course. So Calhoun was happily free of the added responsibility that he dreaded and back on the news rim putting together each night's edition, which is what he loved.

Calhoun even felt relaxed enough to take a couple nights off work because his wife's parents were visiting from Alabama, and she wouldn't let him sleep in the daytime when they were in town. Between the demands of the executive editor and his wife, Calhoun was kept on a short leash, but didn't care as long as he could do the job he loved most of the time.

During his time off, he had watched a lot of daytime TV in and around visiting with the in-laws. He had watched for probably the tenth time a black-and-white Humphry Bogart movie about a crusading newspaperman. Calhoun had been full of the Bogart movie all night, busting to tell its plot blow by blow to anyone who would listen. He was so wound up he kept popping out of the news-desk slot, yelling stop the presses, stop the presses out of the side of his mouth. Then he would chortle and clap his hairy hands and go back to laying out pages.

Calhoun's antics had been getting on Charlie's nerves while Charlie tried to write his week-ender "think piece" on political corruption in the South. He had almost braced Calhoun about it, which would have been a mistake. Calhoun could be as surly when crossed as he was funny when happy.

When Charlie remembered that the independent party's sheriff candidate was throwing a big fish fry down on the levee that night, he grabbed the chance to get out of the news room before he got in trouble. Maybe he could find an angle on the candidate's alleged connection to the local underworld.

Here in the club, with the City Final put to bed, the teetotaling Calhoun was very happy now. He waved at Charlie from his accustomed head of the table always reserved for the newsmen, using his inevitable glass of grapefruit juice full of bar cherries like a scepter, without pausing in his tale.

"… so Bogie pauses, see –" He crouched half out of his chair, building his narrative like some necromancer at a hobgoblin's convention. He left hand clutched an imaginary telephone receiver to his ear; his right held the grapefruit juice.

"So Bogie pauses," he said again. "Then – Wham! He shoves that phone right up to the presses" – a lightning stab of the left arm, with the shadows to his left ducking—" and he says you hear that, mister wise guy? You hear that? That's the final edition, wise guy, and when it hits the street, you're not going to have a friend left in this state. You've been playing my town for a sucker, wise guy, and now it's your turn. See how you like it. So long – sucker!"

The imaginary phone flashed down, and Calhoun's knuckles exploded on the table, sending the shadows grabbing to save their drinks. Calhoun sank back, spent.

"Then what happened, Calhoun-Man?" The amused, indifferent voice belonged to the city hall reporter from Savannah who everybody called Lightnin' Man, for his way with the women.

"Stop the presses for real now," another voice said quietly, with a silken contempt sheathing its non-Southern accents. "Be quiet, Calhoun-Man. Here comes our real-life crusader up to the table round. Or oval, in this case. Belly up, Sir Charles of the White Stockings. I see by the black light of this den of iniquity that you are wearing your bona fides."

"Charlie Boy!" Calhoun's voice still was jolly. "Wet at that fish fry, wasn't it? Fish any good? You gotta big scoop? Got the big dirty? Did the candidate get sloshed and step on his dick with revealing quotes? You gonna stop the presses on the late-night final to replate the break page with his deathless prose? Third horse in a three-horse race admits to sleazy payoffs from Dance Bail Bonds? You finally got the goods to bring The Dancer down?

Charlie sank into his accustomed place beneath the barrage. He gritted his teeth at the Yankee assistant city editor, inexplicably known as Mouse. Charlie hated the baseball-team clubbiness of nicknames in the newsroom. He hated that Calhoun had just extended the nicknaming practice to a red-neck thug with pretensions of Southern gentility. Charlie hated Mouse individually, because it was Mouse who had first called him Charlie Brown, for the hapless comic-strip character, and then called attention to Charlie's habit of wearing white athletic socks with his wash-and-wear suits from Montgomery Ward.

"Think you're cute, don't you, Mouse?" he said now.

"Say rather," the dapper Midwesterner murmured, "I am aware of a certain physical attractiveness devastating to women and disconcerting to men. Right, Angel?" And he passed a hand with loving familiarity over the sleek fishnetted legs of the bargirl who had arrived for Charlie's order.

"Oh you're a reg'lar livin' doll, you are," Angel gave back. "If you wasn't married, I'd rape you right here on the table."

"Do what comes naturally," Mouse urged gallantly. "Take no heed of tomorrow's reckoning."

She sniffed. "Last time I did that, I went PG and the louse went AWOL. You want your usual Bud, Charlie?"

He nodded and she went away. Lightning Man disengaged himself from the long-haired curvaceous woman who sat so close to him that she appeared glued to his hip, and leaned over the table.

"Hey, Charlie. What you doin' still wearing them white socks, Charlie? They're a dead giveaway. If Sweet Thang comes pub prowling after ya, all she's got to do is ask was he wearing them white socks that glow in the black lighting. She can trail you all over the South that way."

"My wife doesn't tell me what to do!" Charlie Brown snarled.

"She sure don't!" crowed Calhoun jubilantly. "Just like mine: she tells you what not to do!"

They all laughed then, because they knew both things were true. Charlie cringed back inside himself. He furtively sought the luminous dial of his watch. He should have been home an hour ago. But the reprobates here would vouch for him, assure Rita that he hadn't been anywhere but here, so he came here and took the nightly ribbing.

Anything to keep the peace, God. Anything! To keep the peace, and maybe let him get a little when she was feeling generous, like on payday. At 29 years old, going without sex was worse than not having beer. He knew this because that was the choice she gave him when they first were married. God, he must have been naive then, he thought. At least he'd finally put his foot down about that. Now he got his nightly beers all right, and maybe sex every other week or so. Somehow she made the infrequency his fault, too. She went on and on about other women, now that he had been transferred to nightside.

"Those night crawlers – those reamed-out whores," she called them. She didn't bring them up when she was honeyfuggling him to get her dress money and bridge club dues and Volkswagen payment. That's what she called it, honeyfuggling. What a dialect pure Georgian was!

Other times, when she was irritable, which was an awful lot of the time, she said he got so much honeyfuggling while working the nightside that he wasn't any good for anything at home. Truth was, he'd never been honeyfuggled by anyone but her in his life, and wasn't sure he'd recognize it if it came his way. The more she warned him and accused him, the more he wished that she was right. He yearned for the casual male confidence of Lightnin' Man or the Mouse that might have made Rita's fears possible.

Charlie didn't understand Calhoun; the news editor was old-fashioned hen pecked, and loved it, or he would have been an executive editor or a wire-service bureau chief in some other state by now. Calhoun was a hell of a newsman, but he needed a hen and a honcho to manage his daily life, and with his wife and the Chronicle's crackpot executive editor, he had both. His orders from the home front were to stay with the Chronicle, not make waves—and absolutely no more alcohol.

Charlie felt himself to be made of better stuff. He yearned for his chance to prove it. He smiled in what he hoped was manly fashion at the good-looking women he met in the course of his political beat. He occasionally tried an entendre when occasion warranted but was secretly relieved when it seemed to fall on deaf ears or was turned into a joke by the recipient.

Ironically he didn't make any such effort with the night-crawlers that Rita feared most. The night people – the tarts and bar girls and predatory women who inhabited this tough, vibrant world that kept a vampire's office hours— would find his soft core too soon, use him and abuse him and then throw him away. He had that much sense.

As long as he was Charlie Brown in white sox, ludicrous but with a bloodhound's nose for news, they respected the armor of his calling. If he discarded that he would never get it back. He had worked too hard to earn that reputation, and it was the only thing in the world that really had any meaning to him. Once he had hopes for his marriage, but those were long gone. The only good part was that there weren't any children to make it tragic.

Calhoun, finished with his Bogart tale, launched into another story, this one personal. Charlie poured his beer into his glass by rationed amounts and listened. Calhoun was a born storyteller. There was none better when he really got going. Now he was back in his cubbing days on the South Carolina beat, covering a moonshine raid in a gas-eating old Buick that had stalled him a mile from Frog Holler.

"... so I decided to cut across the fields to Bath, see. There weren't all them gas stations over there that there are now, but I had a friend in Bath, see, and figured I could make it by dead reckoning –

"Dead is the word, 'cause I forgot about old Clancy Price's plowhorse being all hotted up with spring fever, if you know what I mean. I was walkin' along easy like, see, watching for snakes, an' I kept thinking I heard somebody following me an' finally I looked over my shoulder and man! Have any of y'all ever seen a forty-foot-tall plowhorse with a three-foot-long hard-on, up close and personal in a pasture on a new-moon night ...?"

Laughter. Charlie, too. Calhoun was really at the top of his form tonight. They were still laughing when Pick, the Innkeeper, inserted his sawn-off tenpin shape into the ultraviolet dusk beside Charlie. Pick often came over to listen but he never took the floor, never intruded. He loved the newspapermen because they were free advertising, and a floor show too, and the local cops never messed with a joint favored by the press. The bandits of the press added what Pick's kind of bandits called "class." The newsmen were often into him for healthy bar bills, or even poker loans, because they knew that Pick knew better than to Shylock a reporter.

Sometimes, Pick came to their table with a verbal message or, as now, lugging an ivory phone with a table jack. He called every reporter mister, a pleasing if obvious affectation. When he came with a tip, or with the White Tusk, as they called the movable phone, it generally meant headlines in the offing. Or another lonely woman looking for Lightnin' Man or the Mouse.

This time, the Tusk was for Charlie Brown. The innkeeper addressed him politely by his actual name and plugged in the phone.

"A lady," Pick said courteously, and went away.

"A lady, he says," said Lightnin' Man sadly. "I told you, Charlie. Didn't I tell Charlie, Mouse?"

"You told him, Lightnin' Man," Mouse said. "You told him all along. You told him that Sweet Thang would track him down if he kept on carousing with us bums. A man can't be invisible forever. No man can."

"Not and wear white sox at the same time," said Calhoun judiciously. "I think Einstein wrote a paper on it once. Or maybe H.G. Wells."

Charlie tried to ignore them as he lifted the receiver and waited for Rita's dreaded accents.

"Hello," said a husky voice. "Winston?"

He swallowed his heart quickly and answered in the affirmative. Winston was the Christian half of his actual byline. This wasn't his wife.

"Winston, are you drunk?" The way she said it made being drunk seem charming.

"No," he said, treading water frantically as panic threatened to engulf him. Her voice was making the base of his spine want to wag the tail it didn't have and contract into a spear point at the same time. He recognized the voice—and of course he couldn't remember her name or where he knew her from. Of course.

"I –" He started, and his throat closed on him. He took a gulp of beer and got going again, fast. "No, I'm not drunk," he said. "I mean, a little. I had a couple beers at the fish fry, but I've just started on my first ..." He didn't want to say that. She wouldn't know what a fish fry was and anyway, this wasn't Rita, he didn't have to explain anything. In confusion, he retreated to GI days in Germany. "Wass ist loss, anyway?"

The laughter over the phone was warm and caressing – with a brittle edge he couldn't pin down in his present rattled state.

"You Continental devil, you," she said with a smile in her voice. "I am happening, Winston," she told him. "Everything is happening. Well – many things are happening. Winston, what are you doing?"

He tipped up his bottle and drained the rest of it straight off. The brew feathered over his arid palate and vaporized, with no noticeable effect. He heard Lightnin' Man ask something, from the other end of a tunnel.

Mouse replied: "He's talking to a woman outside the line of duty. That's how he gets when he does that." But she was speaking again, and Charlie was concentrating on her every word as if he life depended on it.

"... Winston, I don't think you know who I am." She was chiding him.

Gently, but that edge was there again. She needed for him to know who she was. Charlie Brown of the white sox was too good a reporter not to hear that in her voice. How many calls from women did he get at the Magnolia Club, she seemed to be wondering. None, not one he wanted to say. Until you. But his mind was still a blank.

"Look ..." he said desperately. "How could I forget you? Your voice still does the things to me it always did." He shut up in horror. Had he said that? If he hadn't, who had?

"Listen to him!" said Lightnin' Man. "You may have underestimated Sir Charles, Mouse."

And then Lightnin' Man winced as his long-haired woman poked him in the ribs. "Shut up, both of you!" she said with a strange fierce protective note in her voice. "Leave him alone!" But Charlie really wasn't hearing them.

Because that ragged edge in the voice on the phone was coming clearer now. "My voice does things to you, Winston? Does it, I mean really? Then why didn't you ever tell me what those things were?"

"I was afraid." That was a universal truth, and out before he knew it. He heard her intake of breath.

"Of him, you mean?"

He was wounded. "Not of him!" (Him?) "Dammit, afraid of you! You know how I am around a woman who I. . ." His throat closed up again. This had to be a nightmare. But she was meeting him halfway, more than halfway.

"A woman that you what, Winston?"

He blundered into it crazily, the pic-maddened bull taking the cape. "A woman I wanted so much. I'm so afraid to show it, I always have been. Because you can make me feel so stupid and clumsy with one look."

Miraculously, there were no more raucous comments or peals of laughter. The cynical crew of the Chronicle melted from around him and he had the table to himself.

"Poor Winston," she said. "So terribly afraid of nothing. Is that really what you were thinking about, those times we were together?"

"... Yes." It was a blanket affirmative to all those women down the years.

The edge in her voice softened. "And I though—but never mind. What are you doing, Winston? Or did I ask you that already?"

"I – I was ... Well I'm having a beer." His body was covered with cold sweat.

"Do you know what I've been doing?"

"No," he said.

"I've been trying to reach you all night, that's what. Didn't they tell you at the newspaper?"

"I'll kill them," he said quietly. "All of them."

Her soft laugh was back, and he reveled in it. "You sound really mad."

"I am. At them," he added hastily, and then found himself laughing with her.

Their laughter died a natural death. The line hummed.

"Do you know what I'm doing now?" she said. Lightly, but the edge was back.

"What?" he said.

"I'm waiting for you to invite yourself over to my hotel room, Winston. I'm coming apart at the seams and I need somebody to thread a needle for me and sew me back together. I need you, Winston," she said.

The image of his wife's unyielding, hard-cute face stood

before his mind's eye like an evil genie. But only for a moment.

"Yes!" he said. "Yes!" then, "Wait! Where are you? The Holiday Inn? Why – why that's just four blocks from here, down Reynolds. What? Room 42? Right! I'll knock twice. What? No, I won't be followed. I – hey! Hey! Wait – no, never mind."

He had cried out when another face suddenly materialized before his mind's eye. A remote, lovely, inaccessible, face saying: "No, I haven't heard from my husband; no, I'm sure he isn't aware of the indictment; no, I have no knowledge of his business connections ..." While Charlie Brown stalked her skillfully, knowing she was lying (thinking she was beautiful), little-boy determined to get the real story about the big man who commanded this lush and loyal creature. And who wasn't worth hanging. Joe Dance, Dance Bail Bonds; the Dancing Man. The Dancer, as Calhoun called him now. A red-neck thug with delusions of Southern grandeur.

"What is it, Winston?"

There was an edge of fear in her voice now. Fear because she had put herself right out there, and now he might back down. Her fear bit at him. There was no way on earth that he was not going to the Holiday Inn, and right this minute.

The Dancing Man's southern lady was on the run. He couldn't imagine the courage it had taken for her to strike out for freedom. But she had. Now she must be on the run, wanting to get out from under Dance's control and afraid she couldn't. But that didn't quite make sense.

Charlie was thinking hard, remembering things now.

No, with her family and connections, she shouldn't be afraid of the Dancer. Her family was Old South all the way, moneyed and powerful, with dangerous connections of their own, and they would not brook harm to a daughter of the clan.

They hadn't been happy with the marriage, but probably figured she'd come to her senses one day and ditch the bum. And now she had. If Dance had touched a hair on her head, he was the one who should be afraid.

So what was she afraid of tonight?

He heard it in her voice, but was unable to credit it. Tonight, she was out there in the night with the rain and her aching loneliness—and she had reached out to him. Him, of all people. And she was afraid that Charlie Brown wouldn't come to her.

"Winston, are you there?" He heard the quaver.

"I'm here," he said. "And I will very soon be there." The joy of being alive and a man sang in his voice. "I'm on my way this very instant. This is me putting the phone down to come to you."

He banged down the phone and almost upset Angel, who was lugging two unopened sixteen-ounce Falstaffs toward another table. Without thinking, he plucked them dexterously off the tray as he headed for the door. He spotted Pick about to open a big brown paper bag at the end of the bar. He remembered in a flash that Pick loved fat delicious jambons from Normandy House, and sent out for them three or four at a time. Charlie Brown shifted both cans of Falstaff to one hand and scooped up the sack on the fly.

"Hey, no!" That genial mobster, geniality forgotten,

flailed his hands after the vanishing sack. "Goddamit!"

But Charlie was faster. Down the bar, around the cigarette machine, out the door and gone. Pick continued to splutter. Lightnin' Man leaned his six-foot-plus on the bar beside him.

"Buy you another ham sandwich or two, Pickster?"

"But – but! He can't …"

"It adds color," Lightnin' Man interrupted. "You know, like if we was cowboys, we'd jump out the window onto our horses and gallop away in all directions."

"Charlie will be back," Mouse said softly, at Pick's elbow. "I'll pay for the sandwiches and the Falstaffs."

"He sho' will be back," called the rattled doorman. "He done gone off in the rain 'thout his fine new London Fog. Or even his hat!"

Calhoun, standing next to Lightnin' Man, swirled his grapefruit juice glumly and speared a cherry. "I just hope the story is worth him catching his death of cold and hell from Rita both."

"Me," said Lightnin' Man, gathering his woman of the moment in his arms, "I hope he gets fucked within an inch of his life."

"Lightnin'!" She elbowed him again, sharply, this time in the solar plexus.

"Well, I do," he grunted. "And the same for me, on a night like this. Let's go, sugar."

Lightnin' Man and his lady passed out into the raining street. Of Charlie Brown of the white stockings they saw nary a sign.

Orphans from the Isles of June

Junkanoo-Time

"YOU GOTTA see it Junkanoo-time," an earnest boatman, selling conch at the Nassau wharf, tells a tourist wearing a straw-market hat, flamingo shorts and green knee-length walking stockings with his black shoes.

"I seen it, man, I got family here." The tourist hefts his Instamatic. "I'll be here."

Wharf Rat's Paradise

SWEET CLEAR DAYS in the Bahamas, cynically called the Bananas by certain grumpy ex-patriates. Autumn days inspire words like hyaline and malachite (kit) in well-vocabularied visitors. The startlingly clear water is polished to a high gloss by the benevolent sun and white beaches in turn are polished by the tides.

This must be the cleanest, brightest heaven in which a common wharf rat ever grew fat and sleek. Perhaps his long-ago ancestors, lean and hungry, swarmed off some pestilential slave ship or rum-reeking pirate sloop, their descendants no more to wander the bounding main.

Near the straw market on a Sunday afternoon you could see them, fat as woodchucks, sleek and bold, foraging for handouts like squirrels in a park. So chubby and almost cute they no longer raise human back hairs in the old instinctive fear and hate. Living here now in a different symbiosis than the London sewers.

The straw-market dollies, always laughing it seems, pause in their palmetto weaving to feed the rats scraps from their lunches. The tourists toss them greasy tidbits of Burger King French fries and Kentucky Fried Chicken from fast-food joints up on Bay Street.

As the sun dips lower, sending golden beams across the island from far west, straw dollies leave their posts to go down to Out Island boats tied to the wharf to dicker over the price of fresh conch and grouper for that night's supper. The tourists evacuate in orderly retreat to gigantic blue-white cruise ships looming over the low buildings on the harbor and the ships depart west after the setting sun.

The sunbeams break and scatter among quiet clean buildings that house representatives of the world's banking industry and tourist shops. On the manicured lawn in front of Rawson Square, wharf rats perch contentedly on park benches and clean their whiskers.

Straw Memories

"YOU WAN' DAT HAT, darlin'? It surely do look lubbly on you. Wanna see a glass?" When the twentieth century still had three decades to run, I wrote that when you heard those words, you're in Nassau, you're a tourist (they know) and you're about to fall under the spell of a straw dolly.

I was living the life of an expatriate writer just ninety miles offshore of these United States. Sometimes it seemed a lot farther from home. We would drive down to Bay Street to watch the cruise ships leave when the weekend was over. Walking in the Straw Market one day, my wife as a joke donned one of the elaborately woven straw hats bedecked with paper flowers. The straw dolly smelled a sale and closed in with the quote above.

My wife hated hats. She almost rebelled at my brother's wedding against an Episcopal tradition requiring females wear hats in church. In the Nassau straw market that afternoon, aloof Norwegian politeness halted Bahamian enthusiasm in its tracks with a courteous rebuff. We moved on.

"It's the camera," I said, hefting my new Topcon 35. "They don't expect residents with cameras."

That day I snapped my favorite photograph of the woman with whom I spent over thirty years: she was wearing a soft slithery dress printed with Bengal tiger. The soft harbor breeze molded the material to her form. I framed her pensive expression behind large sunglasses between dark, primitive, wooden heads a local artisan was chiseling among the straw workers. Her bright dress, long auburn hair and sunglasses among the slightly sinister heads added mystery: goddess of gargoyles.

The photo has vanished in time but I came across faded copies of my Nassau writing recently. When I read the straw dolly's straw-hat sales pitch I could almost smell wood chips from the artisan's mallet blending with the barn odor of straw and sea smell of fresh-caught conch and grouper on fishing boats tied up at Market Wharf.

Nassau may be the only city in the world that lists straw workers with painters and sculptors and consider it an art form. But to me the straw industry resembled a smoothly if leisurely running machine powered exclusively by human hands. As an expatriate writer working for tourist publications I was able to explore the dolly story more deeply than a tourist.

My curiosity took me Over the Hill to the home of a straw worker tourists never saw. At the input end of the Straw Machine, Mrs. Agnes Tucker gossiped with her 84-year-old mother, kept an eye on her grand and great-grandchildren and tickled the ribs of a potcake dog at her feet with one bare toe. Meanwhile, her hands were dipping and passing each other like bobbins in a Georgia cotton mill. A twelve-fathom plait of coconut palm and "silver top" warped into shape as if by magic. Hanging all about her were finished twelve-fathom lengths and batches of raw material.

"Dat silbertop dere hangin', see," she told me as her mother drifted into a snooze in the warm sun, "it still green and bein' cured. I went to duh pine barren myself t'get dat.

One a m'sons, he carry me out dere in his car. But I gather it all. My momma dere, she taught me to plait when I was jus' a liddle girl. Dat surely was a long time ago..." She dipped her grey head, plaited with bright orange wool ribbons, rolled her eyes skyward and laughed. Her hands went right on plaiting without missing a beat.

She told me she never went to the Straw Market herself. She sold her fathoms of plait to a woman who came around to those who prefer to sit home and plait. She then resold it to marketplace dollies who added the elaborate whorls and flourishes and brilliant splashes of color designed to catch a tourist eye and capture the tourist dollar.

The advanced age of the dollies I interviewed, together with the presence of their active parents and grandparents – and youngsters learning the craft – gave me confidence of unchangingness. One of them attributed local longevity to a lifetime diet of conch, grouper, and beans and rice. It was as good an explanation as any. Some things simply endure, like the Rock of Ages. No matter how brief my own sojourn amid the straw dollies, the Straw Market had that feeling of something that would weather winds of change as sturdily as granite.

When I was there the dollies were a fixture, having survived sniping from the "Bay Street Boys," slang for the white party in power back then. Bay Street merchants in their upscale shops resented dollies' competition for the almighty tourist dollar. You could find upscale shops in New York City and London and Paris.

But you couldn't find a living, breathing, wisecracking, ego-flattering human Straw Machine. The market had become the undisputed face of the city. In 1963 the government grudgingly built them the open-air arcade where I found them a few years later, after they condemned the dollies' old digs. By the next decade, a new black-power party that had achieved political control introduced parliamentary resolutions for a fine new Straw Market but it never got off the ground before I left.

No matter how far I wandered later, Nassau remained part of me. Some cities are like that – they stay in your blood. All you have to do when their name comes up is say "I lived there." You will experience a conversational pause as others assimilate this startling statement with surprise, and often envy. Paris for instance – Hemingway called it a moveable feast. Las Vegas – I happened in Vegas, but contrary to the slogan I didn't stay there. Los Angeles, city of angels; I worked there, as *Dragnet's* Jack Webb used to drily intone, though not as a cop.

But Nassau, capital of the Eternal Isles of June, is the crowning jewel of my memory. Recordings of steel-band goombay music I carried away were an infallible medicine for melancholy. Phoenix for example, where 112-degree days made me wonder why I was in a big city in a desert – two of my least favorite things – steel bands could transform the moist breeze from a swamp cooler trying to cut the heat into a whisper of trade winds making up ...

My notes from back then record straw dollies moaning, "Times ain't whut dey used to be. Many's de day I doan make a dolluh." They lamented boom days after the Second World War when American tourists "discovered" the Bahamas—and the Straw Market. This lament was frequent though enormous tour ships called almost daily, disgorging hordes of tourists for whom the dollies were the first things they saw with vacation money burning holes in their resort wear. One dolly confided to me, on what a politician would call deep background, that while she could finish only six straw bags a day to her exacting standards, each winter she sent three or four shipments of fifty or more to Miami Beach boutiques. Her last invoice had been for $800 – U.S., not Bahamian.

The dollies evinced every ounce of the artistic temperament of a painter or a sculptor – —and then some. They were vocal, haggling, cagy, hardheaded, softhearted – and close-mouthed about the bottom line. One said to me: you don't ask a painter what he sold his last canvas for do you? Mrs. Telator Strachan, president of the Rawson Square Straw Vendor's Association back then, told me there were days dollies went home with a hundred dollars.

"Of course that's not every day," she hastened to add, as if she had said too much. "And we have to pay for our materials too whether we sell anything or not. A really exceptional day would bring $150 to $200. But it's chancy."

The sisterhood of the straw was clearly a far deeper thing than just a group with a name and elected president. They looked after one another's stalls, sold each other's goods (charging no commission), tended each other's children and minded each other's business. Nearly all marched together in the Labor Day Parade (first Friday in June in the Bahamas) wearing identical print dresses and— their identifying symbol—straw hats.

Mrs. Mary Thompson told me she always marched. She also told me she could spot Andros coconut palm in a straw baseball cap from across the street, Exuma silver palm in a straw shopping bag, Eleuthera white palmetto in a purse.

From Cat Island, she began to work in straw when she was 13 as so many did—and still were doing, pre-teens learning finger-skills from dollies that would make a Paradise Island blackjack dealer weep for envy. Straw plaits from the Out Islands, like those of Mrs. Tucker from Over the Hill, were shipped in unadorned. When I was there, supply was having a hard time keeping up with the nimble fingers of Straw Market dollies who formed and finished the work with flowers and fish and crabs in a riot of hot colors to mesmerize the tourist eye.

I remember feeling almost proprietary as I wrapped up my interviews and paused to cast a fond eye over the market, running at fever pitch with a new tourist ship in port. Restful tans and browns of the cunningly fashioned straw was accented by explosive bursts of hot color; there were a dozen crooning sales pitches in that lilting Bahamian some first think is a foreign language.

"I made dat hat dere jus' for you, darlin'," a husky contralto crooned in my ear. "I tellin' you nothin' but d'truth, and it suit you ree-e-el good."

"But," I said, "I live here! I'm not a tourist."

"Course you does, darlin', who *wouldn't* wanna live here? Wanna see it in duh glass?"

Nassau Tour Guide

COLORLESS SHAPELESS HAT and suit coat, baggy pants, run-over crepe-soled shoes – he was a dusky shadow beneath the bright island sun amid brightly attired tourists on Market Wharf. Brennan McCurdy, self-introduced, materialized spectrally at the elbow of a straw-basket bedecked stroller who paused to take a snapshot of one of the conch boats. "Dat a fine ex-om-ple of Andros Eye-lun boat-buildin'," he announced.

The tourist had heard of Andros Island, so he nodded.

McCurdy's wide spatulate fingers scratched contemplatively at sparse white whiskers that sprouted on his anthracite jowls like a ghost lawn on a coal seam. "Dey's foah boats interday," he confided in the melodic lilt of a native Bahamian.

After a moment's mental translation, the tourist glanced at the long line of fishing dinghies, gunn'l to gunn'l along Market Wharf near the famous Nassau Straw Market. Customers on the wharf dickered noisily with the boatmen over the price of fresh seafood. "Only four?" the tourist said.

"I doan mean dem *conk* boat." McCurdy gave a dismissive wave. "I mean dem *big* boat from Mi-yammy." He nodded toward tall white-and-blue cruise ships looming over low buildings on the government wharf.

"Oh." But the polite rejoinder was submerged in the sudden tidal surge of McCurdy's analysis of island economic policy: "Widdout de tu-erist, dese islands 'uld be plum ded.

We'd orter make t'ing bedduh foah duh tu'erist." Quickly tacked on at the end of this: "Has you bin in Nassau long, Suh?" Perhaps to indicate there still was a kind of dialogue in progress. How does y'like 'er?"

"I like Nassau fine. You've got a pretty place here."

"Why *thank* you, Suh! I likes 'er fine mysef." Then, a skilled interrogator probing for deeper meaning: "You like d'conk?"

"I've tried cracked conch and like it."

"Does you have duh conk, Suh, where you come from?"

"You see an occasional shell on the beach after a storm."

"Ahhh!" A sage nod showing perfect rapport. "Lissen to what I tel'y'now, cause I tellin' truth. I fish duh conk way down ago. We go outta Nassau forty, forty-five, mebbe fifty mile to get 'im. I hook 'im up, d'conk, long pole, so-o-o"— one gnarled dark hand guiding the long pole of memory above piles of conch shells littering the harbor bottom beneath the wharf, washed clean and pale by the transparent waters—"wid a glass bucket dat ack like uh magnuh-fier. Like you useter lookit duh heb'ums."

"You were a conch fisherman?"

"Way down ago, yessuh. Ain'it whut I tellin' yuh, ain'it? Den I tellin' duh truth! But I ain't nevuh gonna go to sea nomo'."

The tourist was falling under the musical Bahamian story-telling rhythm, hypnotic as the brogue of a story-teller from that other emerald island suggested by McCurdy's name. He knew his place in the dialogue now. "Why aren't you going to sea anymore? Aren't you a fisherman?"

"Nosuh! I wuz, but I ain't now. I only bin off this eye-lund wunce since, and dat was all the way down 1927 when

I takuh boat, go uh long, long way – *long* way – off. To uh eye-lund name Watlin'. Yuh'd call it Selbedore."

"San Salvadore, where Columbus supposedly landed?"

"De same! Dat's de wun. I wuk de rodes dere. Dey was buildin' rodes dere, doe dere wasn't but wun truck on de whol' eye-lund. Dat wun we was usin' to build duh rodes. Some tell me dey got rodes all ovuh dere now. All the way roun' from what you call Ridin' Rock to Sugarloaf, den to duh creek and on aroun'. Some say dat. But I ain't seen it. When I was dere, dey was jus' wun truck." He paused to think on that.

"But when did you stop being a fisherman then?" the tourist asked helplessly.

"Oh – dat wuz *way* down ago, out on the conk groun', y'see. I wuz younger den, and wen I wuz fishin' d'conk, de sail boom come uhroun' and get me – *zwish!*" Two horny palms grazed each other with a rasping swipe. "An' down I went."

"Over the side?"

"Oh, nonono. I too ol' a han' fo' dat! I drop down in d'boat, but wen I come up, you know what?"

"What?"

"Oh – *you* know what!"

"I couldn't guess in a million years."

"Well – I'se been struck blin'! *Thas* what!" He stared out to sea sadly. "An' I been blin' evuh since. An' I aint never goin' on dat sea no mo'. Not evuh! Nossuh! Dat sea dun trick me wid dat boom an' I ain't nevuh gonna give it no 'nother try."

A lot of things crossed the tourist's mind, resentful at being played for a fool by this sharp-eyed old scalawag.

Blind since before 1927, then building roads on San Salvador, and today naming the origin of the very boat the tourist was photographing? He turned to go. But McCurdy was somehow in front of him without seeming to move, talking again, nimbly sidestepping his tale of tragedy at sea.

"You know what, Suh? My mudder, God bless her soul, she still alive. She gettin' on now – I'se got seventy-six years my own self. But she still spry. You bettuh believe what I tell you, 'cause I ain't tellin' you nothin' but the truth." He started counting on his fingers. "I'se got nine chil'run myself. And fo-uh dat die young, doan count dem, dat *still* leave nine. An' *eighteen* gran'," he continued with matter-of-fact pride. "Some of dem doin' quite well but I'se still got uh couple little wuns at duh house. Dey gran'," he added, referring to his mother, "look to 'em while I guides gennamens like yo'sef down the harbor."

"You're a harbor guide now?"

"Yessuh, my t'ird occupation" – counting on his fingers –"fishin' d'conk, rode-buildin', now guidin' gennamens. I puts all the money I gets to buy dem chil'run bread." He paused again. "An' mebbe two cigarettes uh day for me. Jes' two, doe. Ol' man gotta have *some* comfort, doan-he?

Money? This was a new twist. Between his personal tales, it was true, Brennan McCurdy had slipped in that Paradise Island, where the casino was now, was once called Hog Island; and conch fishermen were required to dump discarded shells over there now by order of the government. Because conch shells paving the harbor near the wharf were grounding boats at low tide.

He had described in succulent detail how to prepare conch for eating and waxed ecstatic over fresh-caught grouper. And he had inquired anxiously whether Nassau was meeting his exacting standards for hospitality to tourists; modestly admitting his own hand in the matter if it had.

"Money?" the tourist said now.

"Jes' whutevuh y'kin spare, youh pocket change'll do, Suh.

A bit o' somethin' to get some bread for dem fine chil'run what's dependin' on me ..."

"And a couple of smokes to comfort an old man."

"Yassuh." He cast his eyes down modestly.

"Well ... how's two dollars American sound?"

Brennan McCurdy hid his shock well enough to allow that would be jes' fine, Suh, jes' fine. He even recovered enough to hesitate as he slid the folding money into his pocket, squinting at the green George Washingtons as if trying to turn them into Honest Abes. It happened that they paused for this transaction above another of those Abaco-built boats. Two plum-black salesmen in the boat were dickering with a knot of customers above them. One screwed up his face with unfeigned amazement at what he considered a penny-pinching offer. "Man, dis de *conk*!" he dismissed the unworthy proffer.

The tourist said longingly, "I wish I knew when these guys are gypping me. I wish I could buy some of that without them jacking the price way up because I'm a dumb tourist."

McCurdy had been in the very act of dematerializing from his side, to reappear at the elbows of a young honeymoon couple hand-in-hand in their own little world. Now he reincorporated briefly. "Dey tries to sell y'by size an' not weight," he confided. "Doan let 'em sell you no big shell. Feel if it's heavy. Dat one he fixin' up right dere – dat should go roughly 'bout fifty cent. Lighter brudders go 'bout terty-five, forty cent. He woan sell fer dat, g'won down next boat, nex' man'll sell you."

He offered a horny handshake, and a final "thank you, Suh, thank you – for duh chil'run. Hopes you enjoys your stay, Suh – truly hopes you do."

Then he latched onto the honeymoon couple without missing a beat, already into his spiel. He was awfully spry for someone bent by 76 years and threaded the throng awfully accurately for a blind man walking. The secret of his youthful vigor was doubtless a lifetime diet of duh conk. The miracle of his restored sight was probably marvelous to relate and nothing but the truth, and worth the Abraham Lincoln it would probably end up costing. The tourist was sorry he never got to hear the rest of the tale.

Christmas in Nassau 1969

ZED-N-S plays "Little Town of Bethlehem." Our little Christmas tree twinkles merrily in our one-room "bedsitter." The Police Band was very impressive today. They were changing the guard and serenading the British Governor and the Bahamas Prime Minister surrounded by various VIPs and dark-uniformed police officials in Rawson Square. The sky was wintry and gray, a chill breeze was moving from the bay that lent authority to the myriad Christmas decorations. I shot a few pictures with the Topcon 35mm I purchased from Colin yesterday.

Colin is a Nassau original, short, stocky, myopic and razor-witted; a British ex-pat camera shop proprietor who loves his pint and the companionship at the Red Goat. His hands on a camera are those of a virtuoso. His comments shine beams of clarity into every obfuscatory corner of the high cabal of photography.

"You focus with your left hand, shoot with your right," he instructed. "Hold your left hand under, cupping, instead of over. There are two reasons: your elbows are in close on both sides, and if for some reason the camera slips out of your right hand, it is falling into your left."

The band marched slow-time, wheeling. The drums and horns broke into an unknown number that added crystalline shivers to the coldness of the day. Militant, brittle, the left-rise, left-rise beat of the marching time set

235

the blood astir. The Governor and men in the dark almost black uniforms and British garrison caps were on their feet at once, then the Prime Minister and the other civilians and the women. One of the Bahamians in uniform threw a horizontal blade-edged American salute against his British cap; British crop properly aslant beneath his other arm. The song crashed cymbally to a close, followed by another, softer thing. The music paused, and all the VIP-seaters sat back down...

The P.M. in his dark suit and pink button-down shirt was surprisingly short between the tall rawboned British Governor and his tall lady, in a pink flop hat and English-cut suit with proper hem length, regardless of fad. The P.M. looked – a trifle uncertainly, it seemed to me – to the lank Britisher, like what comes next?

And the band struck up God Save The Queen.

Everyone on the stand seemed rigid for one instant, attention on the Governor. With an exceedingly elegant uplifting of arms that never quite raised his shoulders into a Gallic gesture – and that ended with him standing at full attention – he at once accepted blame for his faux pas in sitting too soon, got back in gear, and invited, almost compelled, the assemblage back to their collective feet.

There was a moment. Colonial ruler and new colonial leader, shoulder to shoulder, surrounded by both retinues. Each as new to these strange islands as the other, in the long window of history. One's people came on the quarterdeck and the other's came in chains, until the Britannic Majesty militated against the slave ships and decreed that chains forged in Africa should be sundered here.

Law and order, a flag that still has a spot on it for a

Union Jack, and some government buildings on Rawson Square; the Queen was paid her due. Then the honorary division commander stood to report his troops.

The governor bent and spoke quietly to the P.M. The P.M. moved out front and center on the podium to accept the honors from that loyal precision. His, now, to command. On his nod, the rest of the ceremony rolled forward.

Orders: open rank, march – the drum major setting the beat with a strictured step. The bandleader behind, rigid, chin at port arms passing in review, absolutely British, tightly constrained within the rhythm. The last song was played slow-march, like a dirge: "Auld Lang Syne." Once down the street, around, the marchers blending and meshing, turning, wheeling, reforming before the P.M. on his wooden stand with the marble queen on her marble throne above his head and the marble leaping fish below him in Rawson Square. Then away, slow-march, with a muted, muted flourish of trumpets and drums.

The natives and the tourists, the expatriates and the mulattos and blacks, the sensitive and the insensitive, moved away slowly, awkwardly. The band's spell faded, rather than was broken ... I went to watch the band and practice my camera work for Junkanoo, the island's Christmas festival, for which Shirrel got me a street pass. We named our Christmas kitten Junkanoo.

Colleen and I went out to Cable Beach and captured it for Wanda. White with a black-and-ginger saddle and a black-and-ginger tail, with a tiny white tip, and a black-and-ginger kind of helmet. She was wild as a tigress when I caught her, looking back over her shoulder as she and her littermates ran from Colleen. Then she was quiet in the shopping bag for the ride home. Then curious in the apartment, then afraid, then hungry, then curious, then afraid, and so on.

"She's so-o-o purty." Wanda was all grins.

Junky has already tried to climb in bed, deduced that the bathroom was where her litter was, and is already used to being handled and demands it by getting underfoot constantly ... now sits on her haunches in front of the Christmas tree, doing light speed-bag jabs with a blue ornament. I feel the danger of becoming a cat person ...

Things have been pleasing this weekend. Up at 4:30 a.m. to go out to Lake Killarney to shoot ducks. No ducks, but I talked with some Italian croupiers from Paradise Island who came to shoot too. They handled their guns with such good manners and such care. I wondered if their fathers had been boatmen and guides on those rich men's duck marshes in Italy that Hemingway wrote about in *Across the River and Into the Trees*. The Italians wore their bell-bottomed hip-hugging gigolo pants tucked into prosaic gumboots, and stylish light wool pullovers to break the chill of a lake dawn. They admired my camouflage coverall. "What do you shoot – a 16?" Yes. "Aren't those loads too light? No high brass?" They do okay, when I have anything to shoot at. "Didn't you see that water hen go right over you?" I try to only shoot ducks. "Ohhh – he only shoots ducks!"

Now my Spanish double stands muzzles-down in Wanda's Norwegian gumboot, shiny slick with WD-40. Zed-N-S continues playing Christmas carols. The neighbor is taking a woman to bed, noisily, after being out all day at a Jack Nicklaus golf school. Wanda gives Junkanoo a Christmas ornament and she pursues it across the floor like a fuseball player driving for a goal.

Christmas in Nassau comes this Thursday, but we have it here Sunday night.

Orphan Stories from the Pacific Northwest

Redondo Reverie

Careless bun of blonde,
Bronze limbs languid in repose.
Iced drink, cigarette
From bay-front porch she watches
Sea-born clouds dim summer's blue.

Country Road Vision

SPRINGTIME IN THE PACIFIC NORTHWEST: today I wondered at the strange closed regal look of ragtag girls in jeans, riding bareback past my house astride fat-bellied, broken-withered horses.

They never fail to eye one levelly and with icy disdain from their saddle-less mounts. They are not having fun, they are role-playing. What fantasy does a swayback refugee from equine recycling represent to these barefoot ragamuffins that gives them such pride of bearing?

September Wind

A WIND RUSTLES AND SOBS around the house, blowing out of the big darkness of the Cascade foothills, reminding me I am not in Los Angeles anymore. I close my book, having just finished a swim in the murky lucidity of Ross MacDonald's prose about Los Angeles, which has new depth now borne of my just-concluded year in L.A.

The names in his story, Wilshire, West L.A., Westwood, call up poignant memories. I can see myself, aged fifty or sixty, as a potential object of attention for the never-aging Lew Archer in some detective story to come. Perhaps as a florid but famous columnist with secrets, a jerky-nerved screenwriter with a past—or a down-and-out bum on Sunset Boulevard. Each witness sneaks up on truth his own way, the detective Archer says in this book. Is that the truth of my future I wonder?

Fastball

TODAY ON THE MIDWAY at the Puyallup State Fair I observed one of those perfect moments. A young man confronted one of the oldest carnival games, the pyramid of milk bottles you try to knock over with a baseball. You have to knock them clear off the stand or no prize, three tries for fifty cents. Few succeed. When I was very young my carny relatives bred my cynicism deep when they showed me every game was rigged. The young man held all three baseballs, selected one to throw and stepped back.

"You're handicapping yourself," the barker said. "You can stand right against the rail."

The young man smiled, took a half-step toward the rail and unleashed the ball. It utterly demolished the stack of bottles, scattered them everywhere. The barker with poor grace hauled down the overhead rack of giant stuffed bears and giraffes and lions.

"Give you two more prizes if you can do that again," he grunted. "Double or nothing."

The young man's blazing fastball demolished the second stack. The two girls with him laughed with delight and selected two more huge fuzzy animals.

Buying coffee across the almost-deserted sawdust, I knew the young man was not a shill. A shill requires an assemblage of gullible onlookers to be tempted into trying their hand. I had been a shill for my carny cousin once upon a time: "If this little kid can do it, surely you can!" Other than participants in this little baseball sideshow, the midway was nearly empty and so quiet I could hear them plainly. Nobody else even noticed.

"That all those things you want?" the young man said quietly.

"We can't carry any more!" giggled the one holding two stuffed prizes almost as big as she was.

"C'mon, double or nothing again," urged the barker.

The young man tossed the third of his baseballs back on the table, slipped back into his jacket. He smiled at the barker. The barker scowled back. The young man walked away with the giggling girls. You don't see many overpowering fastballs like that outside a major-league ballpark. It was one of those small, perfect moments.

Plumb Out of the City

FIVE ACRES OF BRIGHT YELLOW dandelions nod solemnly in the sundown breeze that lifts off the river bottoms behind my house. Beyond the bright yellow restlessness and a backdrop of dark-forested foothills a gleam of evening sun reveals Mount Rainier like God's brassiere through a gauze of rainclouds.

I live plumb out of the city these days; fifty miles to be exact. That's what the odometer tells me, as measured on a winding two-lane through the Muckleshoot Reservation to Interstate Five and from there north to the Mercer Street cutoff to compete my drive to the Seattle *Times* newsroom for a weekend shift as copy editor. People out here usually avoid drives that far. The Queen City might as well be in another state, or another century. Things move slowly here. Life is oriented toward the Northwest outdoors, not the cities of Man.

Yesterday I was in the city briefly, lights sparkling beneath low rain clouds, people all in a hurry; dirty sodden trash whipped by gusts from Puget Sound down below. Now, settling back to slower RPM, the wilderness leans down against my picture window on Mount Rainier to whisper the frontier never closed just because some bureaucrat said it did, little man, peeping out your window.

You can still be surprised and terrified.

Harry the Labrador is preternaturally smart. He pads to the patio door, hackles lifting, and offers a low menacing growl to the bucolic scene. Outraged dogs all over town start barking madly. Horses in nearby pastures snort and mill, then go rump to rump in a primitive defensive circle. What the hell? Coyotes don't merit that behavior. Legendary blue wolves have not been seen in seventy years. There is no living memory of the last fierce griz in those mountains out there. But people who live on this haunted plateau have never doubted the existence of Sasquatch ...

Whatever caused the ruckus goes away. Dogs and horses settle down; Harry goes to sleep. So I ruminate about wonderful morning sex with my red-headed wife and wander around all day with a tent-pole in my pants like some randy teenager. There won't be any doubt I am glad to see her when she gets home from the city.

Orting Crater

WE STARTED OUT with sun burnishing the rain golden; it rains a lot while the sun shines in Western Washington. We rattled past South Prairie in Guy's old Chevy step-side pickup with two motorbikes lashed in the bed. It felt like a whole fresh world with a new adventure waiting. I was young again, or still. I hadn't been old *yet*. The whole earth was green, with rhododendrons, azaleas, tulips, daffodils and who knows what else abloom.

We stopped for coffee in a little café. Cute country girls immediately started talking excitedly behind their hands with sidelong glances at us while guys with them turned self-conscious and wooden, eyes down; keeping a low profile. You would have thought we were flying outlaw-biker colors. For the first time I received "the look" people give you when you have motorcycles. Guy laughed and said you'll always get that look, like you're an outlaw biker, even from people who ride gigantic touring bikes. He *looks* like an outlaw, lean and confident in faded denim jacket and Levis, hatchet face above a rakish beard, roguish twinkle in his eye. Mark, Guy's oldest and beefiest son, wore blue moving-company overalls from his employment, conventional enough. I always seem to loom over my group on any outing and, being largest, draw stares: bushy beard, brown hunting britches, faded Amy field jacket and a Scottish Tam; thick bulge of leather gloves in my jacket pocket.

Finally out into the woods, because these were dirt bikes not road hogs. During the worst of the Arab oil embargo Guy did a hundred-mile round-trip commute on his 250-cc Harley but it's no touring bike. The dirt road was full of deep mud puddles. The old truck splashed into one and stalled. We off-loaded bikes and Guy put me on the little Kawasaki and said he would follow when he got plugs and distributor dry. When I took off, it was cold! My gloves were still in my pocket of course. When I blasted through puddles the spray was shockingly cold and snatched a big burst of steam from the manifold.

With the truck rescued, Guy led out on his Harley, warning that from here on "it's slicker'n snot." He hit a huge puddle and vanished in a puff of steam. I told myself it won't do you any good to be afraid of this damn thing, and wound the little Kawa up. We blew down a road-turned-creek I would hesitate to try in a canoe. I could feel the rear shimmy as the bike clawed for traction. I found Guy waiting for me where the road turned gravel. He was drenched and grinning.

"Good God!" I said.

"Ah, that's not even a challenge for a dirt bike," he said.

He led me across an open meadow. At the far side, the Orting Crater I'd been hearing about all day yawned beneath us: huge, deep, with steep erosion-scored sides; a big dark pool of water far down in the bottom. An honest-to-God crater out in the woods. Nobody seemed to know or care how it came to be there. It suggested to me an eons-old meteor strike; a pretty damn big meteor. We pulled up to study it. Guy told me experienced bikers liked to race around the slanting walls, jumping erosion cuts—but only when it's just muddy in the bottom. Nobody wanted to plumb that dark water with his machine if they lost centrifugal force. Riding up and out is a lark, he said. The very idea made my stomach flip.

He gunned the Harley and roared off for a circuit of the well-worn rim path, itself slanting maybe 25 degrees toward the hole. I took a slow cautious circuit, trying to comprehend the enormity of the thing and concentrate on riding at the same time. All the way around on the far side, the path threads between the crater lip and the edge of a high cliff. The whole Puyallup Valley lay far below in a green shimmer. When I tried to go back counterclockwise the bike got away from me in the erosion cuts. It bounced so hard my boots slipped off the pegs and I landed astraddle the gas tank, crushing my balls so painfully my vision blurred.

I jerked the handlebars the wrong way when I hit the gas tank. Abruptly I was jouncing down the slope toward the steep fall into the crater and starting to tip over at the same time. I goosed it and turned into the dangerous lean, straightened, started to tip again, goosed it and bench-pressed myself back into the saddle, recovered the pegs and rolled out of trouble. Take her around again, Guy said calmly. I was spooked but did it, this time without a fumble. We shut off the motors to listen to the quiet. Far off, hounds were baying.

Guy's head came up like a coyote sensing danger. We better roll, he said. This land is posted and it sounds like they heard us and turned the dogs loose. Hell, so we were outlaw bikers of a sort after all. I couldn't get the Kawasaki to crank. Down the valley, the dogs raved closer. I don't like it that they posted the crater, Guy said quietly. Anything a man likes to do they just can't stand it, and have to post it. Try 'er again.

The little bike came to life on the fifth kick. Off we raced, the hoarse roar of the Harley leading the demented whine of the Kawa, blasting away from the crater. If we could hear the dogs, men with the dogs could hear us. I had that sense of being hunted. We slipped into the muffling trees and up a slippery grade, my rear tire waltzing, and back onto the road. Back at the truck, Guy said the road is public; they didn't post the meadow I guess because they didn't think anybody could get over there from here.

He and Mark took the bikes and rallied down the road, engine noise fading to a mosquito whine. I took a little moment to strut inside myself because I did something I was afraid to do and my skin was still intact. And I got to see the storied crater before it is forever off limits. I sniffed damp trees and ferns and fecund earth with satisfaction. I could hear the distant fury of the dogs at the crater. They sounded frustrated.

Vacation on Pern

WE TOOK THE RENTED CAMPER north to Ross Lake for the first leg of our vacation that year. We got our usual late start and slept in a rest area for a couple hours before I got up and drove on to the lake, which straddles the Canadian border. I picked up a Sunday *Seattle Times* on the way because Eric Nalder was breaking his big story about the covert Moonie invasion of Washington State. He deserved the front page, and got it. He had joked that as Public Records Officer of the Liquor Control Board, I deserved an "assist" in baseball parlance.

He and I spent a day in my office poring through records of a Delaware-registered corporation that owned curb-service stores licensed to sell beer and wine across Washington State. Nalder was hot on the scent, called in by an operator who rescued and deprogrammed kidnapped teens from cults. But it was looking like a bust until we found the name of a Korean CIA official, a known Moonie: just one entry, listed under the ownership structure. There was a routine Liquor Control Board license-division inquiry: who is Bo Hi Pak and what are his financials? The quick reply from a Delaware law firm was just forget it. He has sold all his holdings to an American citizen.

My old reporter instincts tingled when I saw the Delaware registration: back in the day, when I was investigating suspicious corporate activity, Delaware was a known red flag. There were enough corporate "straws" registered there to keep Nassau straw dollies in materials for life. The speed with which the Delaware law firm tried to erase the Korean CIA man from the record, in reaction to a purely routine inquiry, was interesting to both Nalder and me. Doesn't the Bible say somewhere that the wicked flee when no man pursueth? The topless-tavern underworld around Puget Sound had perfected hidden ownerships to avoid LCB license denials. Nalder opined the Moonies had read their playbook.

The topless-tavern mob used straws of their own: ostensible owners with no criminal history. So we took a close look at this American citizen who replaced the Korean. He was very forthcoming about his financial and personal background, affecting a posture pure as the driven snow. He even answered things the Liquor Board did not ask, for instance proudly listing all his social memberships as evidence of his standing. He made one small mistake: one of those social clubs was known to Nalder as a Moonie front in the District of Columbia. Nalder was off and running and never looked back.

Liquor Board officials, jaded by the topless-tavern wars, were skeptical. They had authorized liquor licenses for nearly a dozen franchises owned by this upstanding citizen and social butterfly. Board members considered the stores no more than Seven-Eleven wannabes. I organized a sit-down between Nalder and our lead investigator of hidden ownerships. This man could follow a paper trail like few others, and if Nalder had it he would get it too. I didn't want the Board embarrassed when Nalder's story broke. And it was going to break: one of the creepy aspects was the use of in-store video games to hook young teens, begin Moonie indoctrination, and then spirit them out of state to Moonie compounds. The cult raider's lead had proved out.

For the purposes of Nalder's story, it was enough for me to be quoted as saying we were onto the deception and digging deep. He predicted in print we would find what he already knew about teenagers that vanished into the cult from curb markets we had licensed. Now, in the Ross Lake parking lot, I was satisfied. *The Times* had not embarrassed my agency. I knew we'd revoke those licenses under liquor laws against hidden ownership. Beer sales are the lifeblood of a curb-market, and pulling the license its death knell. I figured the whole operation would dry up and blow away by fall, and I was right.

I was finishing Nalder's story when my wife announced she was taking the kids to ride a tramway to the top of the Seattle City Light dam. I said I want to sleep some more. I put aside the Sunday paper to look into a thick book, *Dragonriders of Pern,* and read too long and slept too little and was cranky when they woke me up, all excited about their adventure. We shopped the City Light commissary for ice and other camping necessities. Headed east, my wife slept across the entire vaunted North Cascades Highway. We stopped at George's Resort on Pearrygin Lake and they put us conveniently near the shower building. After dinner the family went to sleep while I read more *Pern* until I nodded off. It was agreeably cool but green silage being cut in an adjoining field clogged our sinuses.

Next day the kids swam in the lake. I sat in the shade with Mom and read more *Pern.* An admirable vacation book, because all the cult intrigue and other work stress receded into a vacation frame of mind. We elected to stay a second day and went to Winthrop to troop through town. Looked in the art gallery. Shopped in the general mercantile: a plastic raft for the kids; suntan oil. Block ice from the little state liquor agency. I didn't identify myself— I was on vacation! Good hand-scooped ice cream in a little store. There was an old freight wagon pulled around town by small jackasses and the kids got a ride.

I puffed my lungs out inflating the raft—I counted—67 puffs. Then I sat and read *Pern* and smoked my pipe and drank coffee while the kids played on the raft. That night I built a fire for the kids to roast their hot dogs. My wife and I squabbled about how high to keep the fire as we seem to squabble over many things, even on vacation. The kids thoroughly enjoyed some horrid marshmallow-graham cracker-chocolate concoction of hers, melted over the flames. They all crashed, worn out. I sat alone reading by firelight. Work cares were far away. It was wonderful to immerse myself completely in the vividly imagined world of dragon riders. When the fire burned low I doused it and read in the camper. My son came awake enough to whine about the light. I ignored him because it was my vacation too. I was spending it on Pern.

Disturbance
In the Night

I BUILT THE FIRST FIRE of autumn in the fireplace and it drew well immediately. Wood stored in the garage is so dry it burned almost invisibly. I wrote a letter and was working on another when something interrupted and brought home to me how close we are to the mountains.

My wife heard it first, cows mooing in wild distress. The crying rose to a crescendo as if something was into them, and then fell off suddenly. We listened and I was hot to go see what it was but she said no very firmly. I turned on my duck-hunting lantern, but the beam wouldn't reach the back fence of our pasture, let alone to where the noise was. The wind breathed cold. I strained my ears. My wife said the sound was not milk heaviness – farm-raised, she knows that sound. Something was making them afraid. But what? Bold coyotes? A cougar? Possible. Or the baby-stealing Bigfoot of Northwest legend, cousin to the Himalayan snowman?

Absurd thought.

But I went and locked the windows in the bedroom. Our baby son was sleeping quietly. I consulted Junkanoo the cat. She was sleepy, tail curled primly around her flanks. I consulted Harry the Labrador in the garage, curled in a black ball in his blanket. From the garage maybe he couldn't hear the ruckus out there. But he would read the wind with his incredible nose and sound off if something prowled close. He certainly challenges human intrusion readily enough in a roar no one would attribute to a Labrador.

It is good to have the dog and cat to consult. Junky has always been good, her quiet feline abrupt awareness of something warns you without the intruder being warned. And Harry's deep-throated bay might give an intruder pause while I arm myself. Perhaps it was no more than bovine bad dreams. Harry stirs to drink sparingly from his water dish and look at me curiously. Junky unwinds and comes over for an ear rub. Far aloft, a grumbling jet brings a jolt of dissonance to one who has spent the last year aboard continent-spanning flights, and in taxis and hotels surrounded by miles of concrete where a different kind of predator lurks.

City man. Ghetto man. Barrio man. Fearsome enough in their dark skulking, but not causing that cold sharp bracing fear that strikes on the edge of untamed land when cows begin to cry on a forested slope that leans out of the big dark foothills. Cows that seem to cry Man come save me. Man, something is after me in the dark. Man, help me.

Imagination? We didn't imagine the crying. But now all is quiet out there, an eerie quiet after the clamor. I look at my .30-30 leaning quietly in the corner and wish I had gone to confront the fear.

A Happy Little Fish Tale

GUS L., AGE FIVE IN 1975, had no idea what the grownups were carrying on about *this* time when I talked to him by phone from Seattle at his home in Arizona. But he did know one thing:

"I wanted to keep fishing! But they just kept taking pictures and talking. Nobody baited my hook! Mom?" He turned away from the phone. "What was that I used?"

"A worm and a nightcrawler," his mother told him.

Gus had just landed the new record rainbow trout for Lake Powell: a 16-pound, 11-ounce lunker according to the Utah Division of Wildlife Resources. I was tipped off to Gus by a fishing-goods store near Lake Powell. The was family from Everett, right up I-5 from Seattle, in Arizona while his dad worked on a hydroelectric project. That made Gus's fishing achievement a hometown story. They liked to shore-fish Wahweap Bay on Lake Powell. His dad had just baited his own hook when Gus let out a yell. Gus's mom took the story from there:

"He was being pulled toward the water's edge. Jim ran over and grabbed him. There was 4 ½-pound-test line and a size 12 hook on, so he knew Gus couldn't just horse the fish."

Father hovered over son the whole battle, anchoring him to keep him from being dragged in and keeping Gus from tightening the drag. It took Gus nearly a half-hour to whip the fish.

Gus's turn: "It seemed like an awful long time from the time I got the bite until we caught the fish!"

The first thing envious anglers usually ask about a new fishing record is what gear was employed. I put the question to the five-year-old expert.

"A green rod." Gus handed the phone back to mom.

"It was my fishing rod," she said, which explained her familiarity with line and terminal rig. "I've never caught anything on it but sunfish. I guess they call them bluegills around here. My husband calls the rod a nine-dollar cheapo."

Gus wouldn't have to borrow her green rod any more. Jack's Sporting Goods in Page supplied him with a Berkeley 412 reel and Silver Star rod as winner of a local fishing contest.

"Dad thought he might have a new fishing rod," his mom told me, laughing. "But Gus sure set him straight in a hurry. He lugs that rod around with him."

One of those defining moments in a young man's life when the fishing gods reached down and touched him with greatness. Forevermore he would be the boy who caught The Fish. Mere mortals would wonder what was left for Gus to catch.

"Probably hell from his dad for catching the largest fish," said the guy who weighed the fish, with a happy chortle.

Offspring

HE WAS EIGHT YEARS OLD that year. It was before school. He and his classmates were running and crawling in and around playground equipment at top speed. Part of the equipment consisted of the rubber hulks of huge tractor tires. Up and over, around, up and over; burning off energy before they were confined to a classroom.

He landed on one of the tires and started to leap away. His foot slipped. Maybe there was dew on the tires. It was early enough for dew. His foot went inside the hollow tire. His momentum carried him straight on. But his caught leg twisted in the other direction. It snubbed him up short, effective as a leg-hold trap.

There was pain. A lot of pain. His playmates set up a din. A teacher came running. The sight shocked her. She instinctively bent down to pull his foot free.

"Don't!" he commanded.

The strength of his voice stopped her cold. He was small and pale with evident shock. Where had that implacable voice come from? She shook the effect off and tried to be the adult here, telling the boy she had to free him, check him for injury, words to that effect.

"No!" The same unyielding voice. "Do *not* move my leg. Call the paramedics."

She would say later the sheer authority in his voice convinced her. She found it remarkable a child in pretty bad pain had assessed his injury and taken charge of the situation. No thrashing around, no crying—just that unnatural stillness and calm.

Paramedics got there quickly. He spoke to them in that same flat, matter-of-fact-voice, without trace of doubt. He said his leg was "broken pretty bad" to make sure they understood. He lay so twisted it was as if the trapped leg was partly unscrewed from his body.

They got him out of there with professional tenderness and loaded him in the ambulance. Meanwhile phone calls had gone out to his parents. His father – me – was employed in a city fifty miles away. But in one of those quirks that defy explanation, this one day out of the past three years I had been assigned to a town-hall meeting six miles from that playground. I almost beat the ambulance to the emergency clinic and followed it down the drive.

A medic opened the rear door of the ambulance for me. My, son pale with shock, was chatting with the other medic in that eerily calm voice. The medic saw my suit and tie and made a reasonable mistake:

"Here's the doctor now, it's going to be okay."

"Doctor?" Boys don't do eye-rolls as a rule. But he did that day. "That's no doctor. That's just my dad."

A visiting bone doctor brought his drill into the emergency room. He explained he had to drill through the boy's leg to establish attachment points from which to hang weights. The weights would eventually pull fractured bone ends far enough apart they could be realigned for healing. It seemed an awful lot to put on the boy so soon. But the boy wanly said go ahead. The drill was very noisy. Had to hurt. The bone doctor expected tears then.

"Your drill needs WD-40," the boy said with disgust.

They remembered my offspring a long time after that day.

Washington's Lake Geneva

WHEN I GOT HOME last night from Washington's Lake Geneva, fall had come to Western Washington. It rained all day, dead leaves littered the parking lot and trees on the hill behind the apartments were aflame with color. Sunlight had that mellow gold autumn tint. Huge flocks of lesser Canadas arrived in the night, crying in many voices.

I finally visited Lake Chelan. My son called, and had rented a condo there, partially financed with labor-union travel pay, instead of checking into a hotel. As president of his AFSCME truck-driver local, he is there for the annual statewide conference. It tickles me he is backing into white-collar doings almost against his will. It also tickles me he organized his trip to go deer hunting in Eastern Washington, as I organized my AFSCME Los Angeles time to go duck hunting. "Come on over, if you can afford the gas," he said. His wife and daughter went home after they spotted a few does and one spikex2. Beau refused the shot because he wants a big buck; his daughter's doe tag is for Western Washington. He said his wife was all business rousting them out for her first deer hunt with her left-handed 788 in 6mm.

I guess the excitement of my first road trip in a long time kept me from getting sleepy; I was 24 hours awake when I neared Wenatchee. It was the first time I'd seen the vast apple orchards in over twenty years. Dozens of roadside stands, amazing prices – no money. The repaired (by my son) blue Bronco ran perfectly with no overheating. Up the Columbia toward Chelan through high brown wind-sculpted empty hills, I encountered road signs: "Bighorn Sheep Crossing." In all my years in this state I had never been to Lake Chelan. In the town of Chelan I walked Hunter on the beach and she really liked that. I reached the small town of Manson and Wapato Point Condos, fronted by large signs: "No Pets Allowed." Shit, Beau said, I didn't even think about Hunter. I left her in the Bronco while we unloaded; then fixed us a six-egg omelet with cheese and apples from Beau's stash.

We went looking for a place for Hunter to romp and found eerily deserted soccer and baseball fields behind equally abandoned shorefront "summer homes" big as mansions. It was so quiet your ears rang, and the air was breath-takingly clean. On her long lead, Hunter had a fine romp but would not retrieve the training dummy. I shrugged it off, remembering all the times I'd been angry at a dog for acting like that in a new location. This was a vacation! Maybe I've learned something at 68 years old. Hard to believe it's thirty years since Beau broke his leg so badly; repaired later by a top orthopedic surgeon, there are no lasting ill effects. Beau and I had a grand old time reliving past hunts we made after his surgery. I slept badly on a foldout bed, unaccustomed to sleeping flat, while he headed up to scout deer.

After dark I smuggled Hunter inside. I purchased four beef bones from Red Apple grocery store for $1.29 and grilled them. She knows she must stay in her kennel until she has gnawed new, juicy bones dry, and settled right in. She would come out for water and to use her puppy pads, placed on kitchen tile for cleanup. She really is the most amazing dog. She even chose not to bark at strange voices as if she knew we were in hiding. After Beau was asleep she cried under her breath. I let her out. She hopped on the bed with me, curled up and snored happily all night.

I got up with Beau and we put her kennel back in the Bronco before daybreak to avoid any hassle with hobby cops. He went hunting. I slept and read and took Hunter for another romp in Chelan Park, where she caught the eye of a big Aussie sheepdog jogging with his lean lovely mistress. He left her side to touch noses. Hunter thought him quite the fellow. He kept breaking discipline to come wag at her each jogging circuit. His boss never seemed to mind. Finished with her jogging, she came over to ask what kind of dog Hunter is, never having seen a French pointing griffon, and to apologize for hers, saying he is usually much better behaved. She spoke to him severely and he dropped his ears. Hunter kept right on flirting. I told the woman Hunter thinks he is a stud and you can't fight true romance. That got a delighted laugh.

Beau was amused by the story and said the babe had a reason for letting her pooch break discipline, so she could come over and chat me up: Hunter the chick magnet. I'm too old for all that I said, and he just grinned. I did notice she stopped fifty yards away and kept throwing a chunk of wood in the water for her dog to retrieve, turning to look back at me. Beau said she was waiting for me to bring Hunter over. Ah well, I *am* too old, and never knew how to deal with approaches from attractive women anyway.

That afternoon we ambled the high country in the Bronco,

Beau driving, and the differential in four-low. We spotted five enormous mule deer does with truly remarkable ears; something I haven't seen since Arizona. We were the only truck over 27 miles of high winding dirt road, but saw others across canyons. The dry-land canyons reminded me of Arizona, junipers and pines resembled chaparral. When we paused to glass, Hunter snuffled chipmunk tracks in the dust and examined deer tracks with great interest. I puffed my pipe and chewed gum; we went high enough for my ears to pop. I didn't have a license and never uncased my rifle.

The resort itself was peaceful and largely deserted. It was pleasant to sit on the deck with pipe and coffee and watch ducks and geese trade above the lake and squirrels race around the lawns. We watched a World Series game, first ballgame watched together in years. I prepared another omelet, cheese, tomato, apples, onions and salsa. I ate a lot of his chips with his good salsa. He chose to sleep in the following morning. I said why not? How many honest-to-god real, lazy, vacation days have you had since you got married?

I washed dishes and bagged trash and got ready to go. Beau was leaving to finish his union conference work. Going home I spent nine hours at the wheel due to hard rain and roadwork on the pass, then I-5's worst kind of Friday traffic. I was worried about fuel but the Bronco 351 made almost seventeen miles per gallon on cruise control. I could barely walk after the drive. I am getting too old and gimpy for road trips, and spent the weekend nursing aches and pains. But it was worth it, for a fine and totally unexpected vacation at Washington's Lake Chelan with my grown son.

Thank you for reading.

Please review this book. Reviews help others find Absolutely Amazing eBooks and inspire us to keep providing these marvelous tales.

If you would like to be put on our email list to receive updates on new releases, contests, and promotions, please go to AbsolutelyAmazingEbooks.com and sign up.

About the Author

William R. Burkett, Jr. is an acclaimed sci-fi writer, listed in the *Science Fiction Encyclopedia*. But his "straight" writing is a well-kept secret. A product of Georgia and Florida, he now lives in the Pacific Northwest where he can enjoy the fishing and duck hunting. He was once described by author Frank G. Slaughter as a "natural-born storyteller." After a Quixotic career in journalism and public relations, he's now turning his attention back to his trusty typewriter, uh, we mean computer. "Times change, but good storytelling goes on forever," he says.

The New
Atlantian Library

NewAtlantianLibrary.com

or AbsolutelyAmazingeBooks.com or AA-
eBooks.com

www.ingramcontent.com/pod-product-compliance
Lightning Source LLC
Chambersburg PA
CBHW070446030726
47503CB00004B/921